THE DEVIL'S
CAULDRON

SWEPT BACK IN TIME BY THE DEMON BAKA

GARY SCHMELZ

BOOK TWO OF THE JAPAPA TRILOGY

For information regarding permission, please write to:
info@barringerpublishing.com
Barringer Publishing, Naples, Florida
www.barringerpublishing.com

Design and layout by Linda S. Duider
Cape Coral, Florida

ISBN: 978-1-954396-69-2
Library of Congress Cataloging-in-Publication Data
The Devil's Cauldron / Gary Schmelz

Printed in U.S.A.

TABLE OF CONTENTS

Bahamian Dialect

for	fer
into	inta
man	Mon
to, too	ta
than	dan
that	dat
that's	dat's
the	de
then	den
them	dem
there/their	der
there's	der's
there are	der are
there're	der're
they are	dey are
these	dese
they	dey
they have	dey've
they will	dey'll
this	dis
those	dos
today	taday
tonight	tanight
with	wid

GARY SCHMELZ

The Locket

It was hotter than usual in Havana. Captain Pedro Garcia Fernandez wiped his brow and looked around the plaza. There were numerous vendors selling fruits of different kinds, but he was more interested in finding someone who would sell him something that would quench his thirst. Then, he noticed an old woman sitting in the shade of a tree selling what appeared to be small glass bottles of fruit juices. He walked over to her stand, smiled at the woman, and introduced himself. "*Buenas tardes, Senora*. My name is Pedro Garcia Fernandez. I'm the commander of the fleet of ships in the harbor. What thirst quenching drinks do you have to offer?"

"I have many kinds," the old hag responded in a raspy voice. "I think you will find all of them to be very refreshing.

If you would like, you may try a sip from each of the bottles, except for the one at the end of the stand."

"And what is so special about that one?"

"I have set it aside for a friend."

"Then, that's the one I wish to purchase. I'm sure it's the most thirst quenching of the group."

"It is not, Senor. I believe you will find each of the others more gratifying."

"But that is the one I want," the captain replied with a scowl on his face.

"I'm sorry then. I have nothing else to offer you. Perhaps one of the other vendors will have something that will satisfy your thirst."

"Perhaps they will, but I only want to purchase the one at the end of your stand. If it's more money you want, then I'll pay you three times the amount you are charging for all of the others."

Again, the woman shook her head no, with an expression of fierce determination on her face.

"I see," the captain said with a look of frustration. Lifting his sword from its scabbard, he reached out with its point and sliced through the gold chain around the woman's neck and grabbed the locket attached to it. "Now will you give me the bottle?"

"No! You think you are clever, but I must warn you; the locket you have stolen from me will only bring you bad luck. It came to me from a voodoo sorcerer in Haiti. If you want the fleet of ships you are overseeing to reach Spain, you should return the chain and the locket attached to it before any harm comes to you."

"If you think I believe that superstitious nonsense then you are badly mistaken. When I return to Spain with your gold chain and locket, I'm sure I will find a dealer who will pay me handsomely for it and I will become richer than I already am."

"You are a fool," the woman snarled as she gathered up her bottles and left.

"Congratulations on your appointment to commander of the Spanish fleet," the mayor of Havana said to Captain Fernandez when they met in the plaza several days later.

"*Gracias*," the captain replied. "It is a proud moment for me and my family. I am looking forward to seeing my wife and children when I return home."

"I wish I could join you, but sadly I must stay on the island and solve the many problems that plague Havana. Perhaps we can celebrate your appointment together. There is a tavern down the way where we can share a tankard of rum."

Walking to the tavern, the two men shared memories of old times and laughed at some of their narrow escapes from local Indian tribes. Entering the bar, the mayor motioned to the bartender for two tankards of rum and told the captain to take a seat at one of the empty tables.

GARY SCHMELZ

"At last, a few moments of relaxation," the mayor sighed. When the rum arrived, the mayor raised his tankard in congratulation to Fernandez and smiled.

"Where did you get that gold locket?" the mayor asked after finishing his tankard of rum. "Did you acquire it at one of the local shops?"

Not wanting the mayor to know how he really acquired it, the captain said, "I obtained it from one of the local vendors. The man had just repaired the gold chain and put it up for sale with the locket. Would you like to take a closer look at it?"

"Yes, if you don't mind."

"I don't." Unhooking the gold chain from around his neck, the captain passed the locket to the mayor and smiled.

As the mayor closely examined the outside of the locket, his face grew pale and his hands began to shake. There was a carving of a skull and crossbones on the exterior of the locket.

"Do you know what you've acquired?" the mayor asked.

"Just a beautiful locket. It was my intention to sell it when I returned to Spain."

"I suggest you return it to the vendor you acquired it from as soon as possible."

"Why?" the captain asked.

"Have you opened the locket and looked inside?"

"No. Is there a reason I should have?"

Opening the locket, the mayor showed its contents to the captain. "These are the hairs and fingernails of a dead person. This is evil voodoo meant to bring bad luck. The person that wore this locket is said to have great powers. Some say they are wizards that belong to a society whose members are able

4

to change themselves into different types of animals. These animals are known to roam the streets at night and follow those people they intend to harm."

"That's nonsense," the captain laughed. "If I believed any of that stuff, I wouldn't have survived as long as I have. But thanks for the warning. I'll remember it as I sail through the passage between Florida and the Bahamas. There are always pirates after our gold and jewels when we sail through that area, and I'll be sure to keep a sharp eye out for them, especially since I'll have this evil voodoo locket with me."

Returning the locket to the captain, the mayor sighed. "I hope you're right. I only know what has happened to others that have ignored my warnings."

"Don't worry," the captain replied. "I will have four sixty-gun galleons protecting our fleet. If any pirates attack us they will be torn to shreds by these guns."

The sun had set by the time Captain Fernandez left the tavern and walked down the street toward the dock where his ship was moored. After he turned down a narrow cobblestone street, he heard a dog begin to growl at him from a garbage-strewn alleyway. As a precaution, he lifted his pistol and stared at two fiery red eyes that were moving slowly toward him. Aiming his gun, he fired at the beast as it leapt at his throat with a mouthful of sharp fangs. Anticipating the animal's impact, the captain raised his arm to soften its blow and fell to the ground. When he looked up, the creature had vanished. Shaken by the incident, Fernandez stood up and braced himself against the alley's wall. *Is this one of those incidents the mayor tried to warn me about? No. Believing in such things is just plain foolishness. It was a vision created by drinking too much rum.* Laughing to himself, the captain resumed the walk to his ship. Tomorrow, he would be leaving for Spain anxious to return home to his family.

Gentle winds had propelled their war ships and treasure-laden galleons past the Florida straits. Everything was going according to his plans. Captain Fernandez had spotted no pirate ships, and if the weather remained favorable, they would reach the Canary Islands in a couple of months. From there, it would be back to Spain where he would have some leave to spend time with his wife and children.

After taking several hours to rest, Captain Fernandez left his cabin to walk on deck and observe his surroundings. Far to the east, he spotted some small Bahamian islands. He had instructed his officers to steer clear of them to avoid having their ships run aground on the surrounding reefs. He also noticed a band of dark clouds approaching and an increase in the wind. Motioning to his second in command, he told his officer to prepare the ship for some heavy seas.

By midday, the winds generated by the storm had reached speeds that Captain Fernandez never experienced. Huge waves were pounding the ship, leveling its masts and tearing apart the sails. The ship's hull was then struck by a mast torn from another ship. Shouting to two of his officers, Fernandez ordered them to round up several of the crew to plug the hole in the side of the ship. As water poured into the galleon, the captain felt his ship listing to port and was informed by one of the officers that the breach was too large and there was no way the crew could save the ship. Terrified, the captain felt his vessel swept against the coral reef and begin to break apart. "Launch the longboats," the captain yelled to his lieutenant. But it was too late. A series of enormous waves began smashing into the ship, tearing it apart and dragging its crew and valuable treasure to the ocean bottom.

As his ship was being torn asunder by the storm, the captain grasped the locket around his neck and realized he should have paid more attention to the mayor's warning. Now, it was too late. God would not redeem him for his folly and he would soon be engulfed by the ocean and join the rest of his crew on the bottom.

Landrail, Crooked Island, Bahamas

It had been nearly a year since Reggie had met up with Wendell and he was anxious for them to get together again. The wound inflicted on Reggie Sands by the drug-smuggling priest, Japapa, had healed nicely and he had grown into a tall, more muscular young man. Photographs that Wendell had sent to Reggie and Simone revealed he had developed into a handsome young black man with short, curly black hair and a beautiful smile, features that Simone found very attractive. Meanwhile, Simone had become a beautiful young lady. Her sparkling green eyes, radiant smile, and long black hair were features that had started to attract the interest of the local boys who attended the school her father had taken over as principal.

The memories of the close calls they all had with death had not completely faded from their minds, but their lives were gradually returning to normal. Wendell had gone back to New York City to live with his family and attend school. Reggie remained on Crooked Island and now resided with the Haitian girl, Simone, and her family, while he attended the island's local school, and Sharkman had returned to his life as a fisherman and recluse on Fortune Island.

With the approach of the summer break, Wendell had convinced his family to allow him to return to Crooked Island and stay with his grandfather, and his friends were anxious to get together with him. They thought it would be fun to do some fishing on the flats and explore some of the nearby islands. Wendell's parents had been hesitant to let him go, but his persistent pleas finally wore them down and they reluctantly decided to let him go but not before they decided to fly with him for a short vacation.

Several days before Wendell was scheduled to return to Crooked, Reggie had offered to help his uncle bring a wooden chest up to his bedroom. His uncle had purchased the antique in Nassau and Reggie was attracted to the beautiful carvings that covered its outside. "What are you going ta do wid dis?" Reggie asked.

"I haven't de faintest idea," Uncle Lewis admitted. "I was going ta store tools in it but your aunt said it was ta nice fer dat."

"Would you mind if I came back in a couple of days and examined it more closely?" Reggie asked.

"Not at all," Lewis agreed. "Just let your aunt know what you're up ta."

"I will," Reggie replied and took off to meet up with Simone.

When Reggie returned to Uncle Lewis's house and rummaged through the chest, he made an exciting discovery he was anxious for Wendell and Simone to see. He was certain his find would make all of them rich and he couldn't wait for Wendell to arrive to show him what he'd found. He was sure that both Wendell and Simone would be just as excited as he was about his discovery.

After Wendell settled in his grandfather's house with his family, Reggie invited Wendell and Simone to meet him at his uncle's house in Landrail. A loud knock alerted Reggie of their arrival and he jumped off the couch to greet his friends at the door.

"Come in," Reggie said with a big smile. "I've got something exciting to show you. It's in my uncle's bedroom. I found it a couple of days ago. It's in a chest upstairs."

"What is it?" Wendell asked.

"A map," Reggie replied as he led Wendell and Simone to his uncle's bedroom.

"Where did you find it?" Wendell asked as his curiosity heightened.

"In a wooden chest my uncle purchased at a hardware store in Nassau. He said it looked like one his grandfather used ta store his tools in when he was a young man. He agreed ta let me look through it, so when he left fer work, I went over ta his house to check it out. Dat's when I discovered dis map in a compartment in de bottom of de chest." Spreading the faded parchment over the bed, everyone's eyes widened with amazement. Picking up a magnifying glass, Wendell leaned over and used his finger to trace the contours of the ocean bottom outlined on the map. The lines showed the depth of the water surrounding Fortune Island and had illustrations revealing the location of sandy shoals, coral reefs and sunken ships. When Wendell finished studying the parchment, Simone took the magnifying glass from her friend and discovered that the map was printed in 1657 and that the text near its margins was in Spanish.

"Do you know how much your uncle paid for the chest?" Simone asked.

"He didn't say, but I don't think it was a lot. He had it shipped ta Landrail on de mail boat. When it arrived, I helped him carry it up ta his room. My uncle said he wanted ta clean it up and originally planned ta use it ta store some of his tools but his wife convinced him ta leave it in de bedroom to store linens."

"Did you tell your uncle what you found?" Simone inquired.

"No, Mon. When I saw what was inside de chest, I decided ta keep it a secret."

"Why did you do that?" Wendell narrowed his eyes and gave Reggie a curious look.

"I thought it would be fun fer de three of us ta go on our own treasure hunt. If de map marks de location of a sunken ship, I want ta be de first one ta find it. Dat's why I wanted both of you ta see it. I'll need your help ta do it. I certainly couldn't do it by myself."

"I see. And which one of the ships shown on this parchment, do you think contains the treasure?" Simone asked. "There seems to be quite a few of them."

"I believe de one with a cross next ta it shows de location of a Spanish ship carrying de treasure. I suspect it sank in a hurricane. I've already done some research on dis and discovered dat quite a few ships from Spain sank in de Bahamas before returning ta der home ports. And if I'm reading de map correctly, dis vessel went down somewhere off de west coast of Fortune Island."

"What makes you believe the treasure's still there?" Wendell asked. "Someone could have found it a long time ago. With all the sophisticated underwater detection equipment people have access to today plus the satellite navigational systems that are available, it's hard to believe there are any treasure ships that haven't been located."

"I thought about dat," Reggie admitted, "so I talked ta many of de people who've lived on Crooked Island fer de past fifty years or more. None of dem ever remembers anyone exploring de ocean bottom in dat area. In addition, I found another interesting piece of information during our discussions."

"What's that?" Simone asked as she bent over the bed and studied Reggie's map a little more closely.

"I found out dat local fishermen use dat site near Fortune Island to anchor der boats overnight. Dey think it's a good anchorage because der's lots of coral debris dey can hook up ta. De strange thing is, on de recent maps I purchased, dey only show sandy bottom around dis area. Dey show no debris or coral reefs in dis locality. I suspect dese fishermen aren't hooking up ta a reef but pieces of a sunken ship with coral growing over it."

"Well, according to your map," Wendell observed as he tapped his finger on the contour lines on which the ships rested, "the water depth in that area off Fortune Island is a little over thirty feet. If that's the case, you're going to need scuba gear to explore the bottom and I, for one, am not a certified diver."

"Mon, don't worry about dat. With some of de money I collected from my parents' life insurance policy, I was able ta purchase some second-hand scuba equipment in Nassau. Simone and me have been testing it out in 30 feet of water near Landrail. So far de gear seems ta work fine. I'm sure we won't have any problem using it ta search fer de wreck. My uncle also bought me a hand held GPS which I intend ta use ta mark de location of de sunken vessel once we find it."

"I thought your folks didn't have an insurance policy," Wendell said with a surprised look.

"Dat's what I thought ta," Reggie admitted, "but it turned out my dad took out a small policy a short time before his death. My uncle learned about it when he went through my father's papers, and he passed de money on ta me."

Still skeptical, Wendell nodded his head and took one last look at the map. "It sounds like a plan, but you'll need a vessel bigger than the *Sea Star* to carry out this operation. Your boat is way too small to conduct this type of work. Another problem could be the fishermen that are working in that area. They might become suspicious about what we're up to."

"I intend ta tell de fisherman we are just looking fer lobsters and doing some underwater photography. But I haven't quite worked out de problem of de boat. I was hoping ta convince Sharkman ta let us use his vessel fer a couple of days."

"I think that might be possible." Simone smiled. "I talked to him the other day when he was in Landrail and I asked him if Reggie and I could use his boat to harvest lobster. He was a little hesitant at first but agreed he'd let us do it when he found out we were only going to take it a short distance from where he lives on Fortune Island."

"Dat's great!" Reggie wrapped his arm around Simone and gave her a big hug. "Now all we have ta find is some equipment we can use ta haul any treasure we find aboard."

"What do you think about Reggie's plan, now?" Simone asked Wendell as she reached across the map and took hold of his hand.

A little flustered when Simone reached out and affectionately squeezed his hand, Wendell blushed and nodded his head in agreement. "The idea is exciting, but I have some reservations. I especially don't like the idea of deceiving Sharkman. If he finds out about what we're using his boat for, he's going to get really upset."

"Mon, he won't find out." Reggie waved his hand in frustration and shook his head. "Like Simone says, he thinks we'll be going after lobsters. We can even bring him back a couple ta eat after each day's outing."

"That settles it then," Simone said as she jumped up and gave Reggie and Wendell a kiss on each of their cheeks. "I can't wait for us to get started. Just think, we might all become very rich."

"Perhaps," Wendell grumbled, "but I still think the plan's a little risky. Besides, what are you going to tell Simone's mom and dad? I don't think they'll be very excited about the two of you scuba diving for lobster without Sharkman along. My folks are here for a week visiting my grandfather and they will also want to know why I'm not spending more time with them."

"Dat's a good point," Reggie admitted and paused a moment to reflect.

"We'll tell them it's nothing to worry about because Sharkman will be watching over us and that Reggie and I merely want to learn about his fishing techniques," Simone suggested.

"Good thinking," Reggie replied. "I will bring it up wid your folks tanight. I'm sure it'll work. Meanwhile, Wendell, you can tell your folks dat Sharkman is teaching de three of us ta lobster and how excited you are ta learn how ta do it."

"More lies. Eventually, they're all going to find out what we're up to and there's going to be you know what to pay for it. In the end, lies always get you in trouble. And, where do you plan to refill your tanks?"

"I don't think we'll have to worry about that. I think Sharkman has a small compressor to refill them at his place," Simone noted.

"Don't be such a wimp," Reggie grumbled. "Once we make our families rich, none of dem will care what we've been up ta."

"So you say. I guess we'll just have to wait and see how this whole plan of yours works out. I still think it could get us into serious trouble." Wendell sighed as he reached up to his neck and without thinking began fondling the amulet Simone had given him. After their near fatal encounter with Japapa, Simone said it would prevent bad things from happening to him. She told him it was given to her by a powerful voodoo priestess she trusted with her life. Thinking about Reggie's proposal, he hoped the amulet's ability to protect him still worked.

As Reggie began rolling up the treasure map, Sharkman's parrot landed on the bed and began to chew on the end of the parchment paper. Afraid that the map might get damaged, Reggie swatted the bird and was relieved to see it fly out the window and land on a nearby tree. "Dat bird is a real pest. I should have left him home. Now I know why Sharkman gave it ta me," Reggie grumbled.

"Danger, danger," the bird squawked.

"Yeah, yeah, you're always crying 'danger'," Reggie grumbled. "De only thing in real danger is you, because de next time you begin squawking like dat, you'll be de one dat will be in trouble."

It had been a year since the demon, Baka, had last seen the trio from Crooked Island. As Baka listened in on Reggie's plans to retrieve treasure from a sunken galleon, he sat back, grinned, and thought, *The time has come to initiate my plans for revenge. I will need someone to help me of course, but that will be easy with so many to choose from in Hell.*

Soon, Sharkman and the youths will be swept up into a terrifying nightmare that would destroy the spirit of any mortal. And when it's over, they will all beg me to let them die. My only concern is the old woman. Mama Atabei, the Haitian priestess, has upended many of my plans in the past. This time, however, I believe I've come up with a way to remove her from the equation.

Treasure Hunting Begins off Fortune Island, Bahamas

The next morning Reggie and his friends loaded the *Sea Star* with their diving equipment and extra gasoline and took off to Sharkman's residence on Fortune Island.

Sharkman was still sleeping when the youngsters knocked on the door of his hut and woke him up. "Who is it?" he asked as he lifted himself up from his cot, scratched the stubble on the end of chin, and matted down the grey hair on the top of his head.

"It's Reggie," the boy shouted loud enough so the old man could hear him.

"What do you want?" Sharkman asked as he opened the door to his hut and was greeted by Reggie and Simone's smiling faces.

"We'd like ta borrow your boat fer a couple of days ta go lobster fishing," Reggie said. "Is der any chance you could let us do dat? Simone said she talked wid you about it and thought you might be agreeable. We only want ta hunt fer lobsters near here and we'll bring you back some fer dinner."

"Why don't you use your own boat or borrow your uncle's?" Sharkman wanted to know as he put on an old pair of fishing pants he had patched up the previous night.

"Mine is ta small ta dive off of and my uncle is using his ta go fishing wid friends."

Sharkman was reluctant to let the teens use his boat but their promise to stay nearby and bring home some lobsters for dinner weakened his resolve. "You can use my boat, but make sure you take care of it and have it back before sunset. Also, make sure you fill up the gas tank."

"Thanks, we will," Reggie replied.

Sharkman reached into his pocket, pulled out his boat key, and gave it to Reggie. Smiling, Reggie and Simone thanked the old man then raced down his dock to meet up with Wendell and begin loading the fisherman's boat with their diving equipment. It only took the teens a few minutes to pack their gear on the boat and take off toward the north end of Fortune Island. The surrounding waters were calm as the youngsters disappeared behind a line of Australian pines.

Sharkman wondered what they were really up to. He was sure he would soon find out. But for now, he appreciated the break in fishing. He needed some time to repair his tackle and mend his nets. The last few weeks of fishing had taken its toll on his equipment and if he was going to be able to catch enough fish to sell at the local market, he needed to unpack the supplies he'd picked up in Landrail the other day and begin work on his gear.

"How do you think he felt about us using his boat?" Wendell asked Simone as Reggie entered the GPS location in his device.

"I think he was a little suspicious," Simone replied, "but when Reggie promised him that we would stay nearby and only wanted to collect lobsters, he relented."

"I think when we promised ta fill his boat wid gas also helped him make up his mind," Reggie added.

"We should reach de site of de sunken ship in about twenty minutes," Reggie shouted to his companions as Sharkman's vessel chugged along. "If you'd get de diving gear out of de cabin, Simone, we could begin searching fer de sunken ship as soon as we get der."

"Ok," Simone shouted back as she entered the boat's cabin to pick up the equipment.

It was the perfect day for diving. The smooth, emerald green waters surrounding Fortune Island were crystal clear. Reggie judged the visibility in the vicinity of the sunken ship was going to be about fifty feet and he was anxious to put his gear on and begin diving. His GPS soon indicated he was close to the wreck, so he slowed the boat's engine and checked the vessel's bottom finder. It was beginning to show just the right kind of ragged bottom he was hoping for. "Head ta de bow and get ready ta throw over de anchor," Reggie shouted to Wendell.

Crossing over what appeared to be a pile of rubble, he turned the vessel around and examined the bottom contour a second time. He wanted to make sure what he was looking at wasn't a patch of live coral. If it was coral, it was not the site they were looking for, and throwing the anchor out would damage a valuable marine habitat. Unfortunately, the image on his depth finder revealed that they were not over a sunken ship but a small patch reef, so he guided the boat into slightly deeper water and maneuvered it until he found what appeared to be a rocky ledge with an unusual structure situated near the top. At that point, he signaled Wendell to cast the anchor over. Within seconds of reaching the bottom, its pointed flukes grabbed hold of the ledge and the boat swung into position. Once it was secure, Reggie turned off the engine and Simone threw over their dive flag to warn other boats in the area to steer clear.

"Let's go," Reggie shouted as he moved toward the rear of the vessel and he and Simone began putting on their diving equipment. "De structure we're going ta look at is in about 40 feet of water," Reggie informed Wendell. "Dat's a little deeper dan Simone and I usually dive down ta, but we should be ok."

"How long will you be down there?" Wendell asked apprehensively as he watched his friends finish putting on their equipment and prepare to jump overboard.

"Hopefully not more dan 45 minutes," Reggie said. "My uncle gave me a diver's watch fer my birthday, so I'll be able ta keep track of time. If we find something, I'll take a GPS reading when I return ta de surface."

"Are you guys finished talking?" Simone chided. "We'll never uncover anything if we don't get going soon."

"Nag, nag, dat's what women do all de time," Reggie teased. He hoisted the tank on his back and once secured, he put on his face mask and flippers. He perched himself on the gunnel and then flipped over backwards into the water. A few seconds later Simone followed.

After Wendell watched his friends disappear toward the bottom, he headed to the boat's bottom finder. It revealed several mounds of rubble that he assumed were parts of the sunken Spanish galleon he'd seen marked on the map. It shouldn't take them too long to reach the debris and report back about what they'd found. Nevertheless, 45 minutes seemed like an eternity and it felt like it was taking forever for his friends to return. As he stared into the crystal-clear water, he spotted Simone and Reggie waving to one another. Simone had two lobsters in tow while Reggie was carrying a encrusted stick-like object. When they surfaced at the rear of the boat, Wendell quickly leaned over the side, took the lobsters from Simone, then grabbed the rod-like structure from Reggie.

"Take dese as well," Reggie shouted and passed his flippers and facemask up to Wendell and slowly climbed up the ladder at the rear of the boat.

After tossing the two spiny crustaceans into an empty wooden box, Wendell returned to help his friends finish removing their gear.

As Wendell placed the encrusted object on the deck, he asked, "Is this the only thing you found?"

"I think it's de remains of Spanish sword," Reggie said excitedly.

"Did you see any gold and silver coins?" Wendell asked.

"None. But I'm sure dis is de place de Spanish ship went down and I'm sure it's de ship dat's marked on de map."

"How about you? Did you see any coins or jewelry?" Wendell inquired of Simone.

"You seem awfully anxious about us finding treasure," Simone laughed. "The truth is I didn't see anything valuable lying on the bottom. However, there were a lot of lobsters hiding in the debris piles we swam around."

"I suppose that was good," Wendell responded. "We'll need a few more of them if we're going to bring back the meal we promised Sharkman. In the meantime, I'd like to take a closer look at the sword, Reggie."

"So would I," Simone said and followed Wendell over to where Reggie was sitting on the deck admiring his find. "Do you think it was used by one of the ship's crewmen?" she asked while bending over to take a closer look at the barnacle encrusted blade and handle.

"I'm sure it was," Reggie replied. Handing it over to Wendell, he cautioned him to handle it gently.

"You can barely make out what it is," Wendell replied as he brought the object closer to his face.

"Should we clean it?" Simone asked.

"I wouldn't do that," Wendell interrupted. "Cleaning artifacts is a very delicate process and if you make a mistake you could seriously damage it. It's a job that should be undertaken by a specialist in a museum. Some of the books I've read about preserving artifacts say the best thing to do now is place the sword in a sealed container of sea water. If you let the object dry out, the salt inside it will crystalize and the object will disintegrate from the inside out leaving behind a pile of orange dust."

"I suppose we should do what Wendell suggests," Simone said, as Wendell gently handed the sword back to Reggie

"He's right," Reggie acknowledged. "I've heard some of de same things about preserving artifacts. It's a pity we can't clean it right away. I know der's no one locally dat can clean it, but I do know some people at de pirate museum in Nassau. Dey might be able ta clean de sword, and if dey can't, dey might be able ta contact someone who can. My uncle could also help us by bringing some of de other things we uncover to de museum for cleaning."

"Sounds like a plan to me," Wendell replied. "Are you and Simone going to make another dive?"

"Yeah. I brought two extra air tanks. We'll pick up some more lobsters fer Sharkman. We can't go back wid just two and while we're down der we'll also look fer some more artifacts."

"Maybe we'll find some gold and silver coins while we're at it," Simone added with a grin.

"Hopefully," Reggie smiled while he prepared their gear for the next dive.

The second dive produced plenty of lobsters but only one additional artifact, a silver spoon Simone uncovered amid some coral rubble.

"I've been thinking," Reggie said after he boarded the boat and Simone retrieved the dive flag. "We should have found more artifacts on de bottom dan we have. It could be dat de hurricanes dat passed through dis area since de ship sank have spread de remains of de ship over a much wider area. If dat's de case, den we are going ta have ta come back a lot more times dan I anticipated and broaden our search area."

"You're probably right," Simone agreed, "but Sharkman isn't going to let us use his boat that often. He'll soon need it to catch fish. What do you suggest we do?"

Starting up the engine, Reggie took a moment to reflect as they headed back to Sharkman's dock. "Maybe we could use my uncle's boat when he's not out fishing with his friend next week. I could ask him if we could borrow it ta go diving. Since he doesn't have a lot of money, we'd have ta pay fer de gas. De only way I can think around dat problem is ta catch more lobsters while we're looking fer treasure and sell dem ta de local resorts. Dat should give us de money we need fer fuel."

"Good idea," Wendell agreed. "When do you think your uncle can take the artifacts we found up to Nassau?"

"He only goes ta Nassau once a month, so it'll be a couple of weeks before he heads up dat way. I'll tell him I found dem while we were lobster fishing wid Sharkman's boat."

"That's a pretty long time," Wendell frowned. "In the meantime, we'll need to store what we find someplace where no one will discover it. Do you have a place in mind where we might do that?"

"Not really. We can't bring dem back ta Sharkman's place or our houses. However, I do remember a cave my father and

25

I discovered a couple of years ago when we spent some time exploring Fortune Island, and it's not ta far from here."

"I hope it's not the cave Japapa kept me captive in. That place gave me the creeps." Simone shivered as she thought back to her experience with the evil voodoo priest.

"I'm sure it's not. De cave we found was nowhere near Japapa's camp. It's only a short distance from here. We can look at it before we head back ta Sharkman's place, and if it turns out ta be a suitable location, we could drop off de artifacts we found taday."

Let's look for it," Wendell said. "We have a few hours before the sun sets."

After listening in on the teens' conversation, Baka smiled with anticipation. *The butterflies are about to become ensnared in my web. I can't wait to see how they will struggle to free themselves from the trap I'm setting. Few, if any, have ever escaped alive from my clutches.* The satisfaction his plan gave him made him tremble with joy.

There is one more thing: to make sure Mama Atabei doesn't interfere with my plans, I'll create a catastrophic event in Haiti. It will generate pleas for help from the natives of her home country and it will be something she won't be able to ignore. Once she realizes she has been tricked, it will be impossible for her to help the youngsters or Sharkman.

As Baka sat in his cozy, fiery den and surveyed his kingdom of suffering souls who were constantly crying out in pain, he smiled with delight.

Looking for a Hiding Place

Altering his course, Reggie guided the boat about a half mile farther down the beach and moved it as close to shore as he could without running aground.

"Dis should be de place," Reggie said as he ordered Wendell to throw the anchor over. "De cave is about a quarter mile from de beach up dat hill in de distance. I'll grab de satchel we placed de artifacts in and lead you ta it."

The cave turned out to be farther from the beach than Reggie remembered, and Wendell was panting by the time they arrived at the crest of the hill where the cave was supposedly located. "How much further do we have to go?" he complained.

"You city wimps are all de same," Reggie laughed. "I doubt you would survive more dan a week if I left you alone on one of dese islands."

"Ha, ha," Wendell retorted. "If you remember correctly, I'm the one that saved your butt on Castle Island."

"I don't think you'll ever let me forget dat," Reggie grumbled.

Simone shook her head when she reached her two companions. "Are you two finished trying to prove who is more macho than the other? We need to find this cave you talked about, Reggie, and get back to Sharkman's hut before the sun sets. I, for one, don't want to be out here wandering around in the dark looking for it."

"Ok. We're almost der. I think it's hidden behind dat cluster of gumbo limbo trees about a hundred feet from here, but go slow when you come out of de bushes. Der is a steep drop on de other side dat leads ta de cave's entrance and de rocks leading down ta it can get slippery."

Reggie was right about the rocks being slippery and both Simone and Wendell had a difficult time crawling over them to reach the entrance of the cave. When they arrived, everyone took a moment to recuperate and enjoy the view.

Over the years, rainwater had seeped into the lime rock that formed the crest of Fortune Island creating a magical place Reggie said few of the local islanders knew about. Near the mouth of the cave, a turquoise blue pool of water reflected the cave's entrance and the surrounding tropical vegetation. It was a breathtaking site that Simone and Wendell realized they would never forget.

29

"Beautiful isn't it? It was one of my favorite places ta visit when I went out exploring wid my father before he was killed." Reggie wiped a tear away from his cheek and sighed. "We learned dat stray goats and pigs would come down here ta drink from dis pool during de winter dry season, and my father and I like ta bathe in de cool water during de warm summer months."

Beyond the pool of water, the cave's wide entrance was almost completely covered by a carpet of morning glory vines whose purple flowers added to the site's beauty. "You're right; it's a beautiful location." Simone sighed as she took a moment more to enjoy her surroundings before heading off with the boys into the cave's entrance.

Once inside the cave, the trio of fortune hunters was quickly engulfed by its dark interior. "W-what's that squeaking sound?" Simone stammered after her eyes adjusted to the darkness. Shaking, she grabbed ahold of Wendell's arm.

"Bats," Reggie replied. "Der are thousands of dem hanging from de ceiling. Dey rest here during de day and leave de cave at night ta capture food."

"This is also one of the worst smelling places I've ever been in," Wendell complained.

"I'm afraid you're going ta have ta get use ta da stink if we decide ta hide our treasure in here. You're smelling bat shit."

"You mean bat guano," Simone said in disgust.

"Well-yeah. I guess dat would be de polite way of describing it. We're probably standing in some of it right now." Turning on the mini-flashlights they purchased at the general store in

Landrail, Simone and Wendell watched in shock as dozens of large cockroaches scampered across their feet and up their legs.

Letting go of Wendell's arm, Simone yelped and brushed away the roaches crawling up her legs. "Get them off of me!" she screamed.

"Dey won't hurt you," Reggie laughed as he and Wendell helped brush them off her legs. "Dey are only bugs and dey don't bite."

"So you say," Simone shivered. Brushing off several more large roaches crawling up her legs, she stomped on them and wrinkled her nose when the sweet smell of their crushed bodies seeped into her nostrils. "I'm never going in here again," she shouted defiantly and folded her arms against her chest.

"Sorry," Reggie said when he and Wendell finished wiping the bugs off her. "But dis is de only place I could think of ta hide de treasure. None of de local islanders know dis place exists and even if one of dem found it, I doubt dey would spend ta much time looking around inside."

"I can see why," Simone grumbled.

"I'll tell you what. Wendell and I will bring whatever treasure we find inside de cave. All I'm asking you ta do is ta help us bring it ta de cave entrance and wait fer us outside."

"I suppose I can do that," Simone relented.

"Do you have a location in mind where we could stash the artifacts?" Wendell asked.

"Not really," Reggie admitted. "But it shouldn't take ta long ta find one. We obviously need a place where de artifacts can stay relatively dry. In addition, it should also be a spot where someone who might explore dis cave couldn't find dem. While we're doing dat, Simone can remain outside as a lookout."

"It's dark in there. Did you bring some stronger flashlights?" Wendell asked.

"As a matter of fact, I did," Reggie boasted as he reached into his backpack and pulled out two large ones and handed one to Wendell.

"Great," Wendell said. Testing the one Reggie had given him, Wendell smiled with relief as the new flashlight cast a bright light into the cave's interior.

"Satisfied?" Reggie rolled his eyes and laughed. "I made sure I tested dem before we left. Let's get going. De sooner we find a spot, de sooner we can head back ta Sharkman's place. It'll soon be dark, and I don't want him ta start worrying about us."

Footing was treacherous inside the cave. Water seeping from the ceiling caused them to slip and fall several times as they slowly made their way further into the cave's dark interior. After slogging their way through a chilly stream, Reggie suggested they leave the shallow waterway and climb upwards through a maze of stalactites and stalagmites to a chamber he'd discovered when he'd explored the cave with his father. It took them several minutes to reach the spot Reggie was looking for and both boys were exhausted by the time they arrived at his destination.

"Do you think dis is a safe enough place ta hide de artifacts?" Reggie panted and shined his flashlight into a large, empty chamber.

Wendell nodded in approval. "I do." Using his flashlight to further examine the area where Reggie planned to store the treasure, he smiled with satisfaction. "This place looks ideal. It's dry and reasonably close to the cave's entrance, but also tucked far enough back so no one will find it. Besides that, it's very spacious so we can store a lot of the treasure here, and it's high enough so it won't get damaged if the cave gets flooded. What about the artifacts you found today? Do you think we should leave them here before we head back to Sharkman's place?"

"That was my intention," Reggie nodded. "I can't wait ta see what other discoveries we will make tomorrow. I have a feeling we're all about ta become very, very rich."

The demon Baka watched the youngsters in the cave and chuckled to himself. There was no way they were going to become rich. A comforting feeling seeped into his body as he imagined the future he had in store for them. Not today though, or even the next few. *First, I will let them feel how gratifying greed can be. Money will soon begin to mean everything to them. They will begin to think of all they can do with their newfound riches like Reggie building a new house or the group purchasing a dive boat.*

Sharkman, however, is another matter. He can't be enticed by greed. His weakness lies in his desire to protect the natural resources of the Bahamas and his insistence on protecting the sacred temple he discovered in Vietnam. I've tried many times to pry the location of the temple from him, but each time I failed. This time I will be successful. As he mused over this matter, a wicked thought came to him, one that would enable him to extract the temple's location. The plan was so fiendish, the excitement it generated was hard to control. *Tomorrow I will think about a way to carry it out.*

Fortune Island–Treasure Hunting
Day 8

"So, you thought we're going to become very rich," Wendell grumbled. "We've been exploring this area for over a week and we still haven't found any treasure. So far, the only thing we've uncovered are lots of broken pieces of pottery, some more silver spoons, a few knives, several cannon balls, and a ship's anchor, and we don't have the equipment we need to bring all of it to the surface."

"I know, I know, Mon, but we can't lose faith. De treasure chest we're looking fer has ta be close ta here. Dos things dat we've found are surefire indicators dat we're close ta finding it."

"I hope so. We spent a lot of time using Sharkman's boat and now your uncle wants his boat back so he can go fishing with his friend, and we still haven't caught and sold enough lobsters to pay for the gas that we've used."

"I agree with Reggie," Simone said. "We need to look on the bright side. Each day we seem to be finding more and more artifacts which suggests to me that we're very close to locating the treasure. I have a good feeling about this dive we are about to make."

"All right," Wendell conceded. "But I sure wish we'd find some treasure soon so my faith in this undertaking will improve."

"We will," Simone assured him as she and Reggie flipped into the water and headed toward the bottom.

The water in this area was murkier than the other sites they explored. When they reached the bottom, Reggie and Simone headed toward a jumbled structure protruding from the seagrass bottom. Even when they got closer, it was hard to tell what the tangled mass was. It could be the ship's cabin but it was hard to make it out because it was covered with a forest of purple sea fans and sea whips. There were also large schools of fish surrounding the vessel. Blue tangs and small mouth grunts were everywhere, and several feet from a hole that could be the cabin, they encountered an enormous grouper and a large moray eel. After spending some more time swimming around the structure, Reggie motioned to Simone to head toward the surface.

"What do you think it is?" Simone asked Reggie when her head bobbed above the surface and she removed her face mask and mouthpiece.

"With all de marine life clinging ta it it's hard ta tell," Reggie replied after removing his mouthpiece. "It doesn't look like any of de pictures of sunken ships I've ever seen in books."

"But it could be the one we're looking for."

"It could be. But it'll be spooky trying ta explore de insides of dat twisted mass. Did you see de mouth on dat grouper? He must weigh over 600 pounds. Guess dat's why dey call it a goliath grouper. And dat moray eel was huge. My guess is dat he's five feet long and almost as thick around as your leg."

"What do you think we should do?"

"I guess we don't have any choice. If we are going ta find de treasure, we're going ta have ta see if der is anything hidden in der. But I'm not going in der without some protection. I'll get my speargun from de boat just in case one of dem large fish decides ta attack us." Lifting off his face mask, Reggie shouted and waved to Wendell to give him his speargun.

"What's up?" Wendell asked as he picked up the speargun.

"It looks like we found part of de ship we've been looking fer but der are some nasty looking creatures lurking around it. One's a huge goliath grouper and de other is an enormous moray eel. If we hope ta get inside de ship and check it out fer treasure, I'm going ta have ta make sure we have some way of protecting ourselves."

Wendell leaned over the boat's gunnel and handed Reggie his speargun. "Good luck," he shouted to Reggie and Simone before they replaced their face masks and returned to the bottom.

As they approached the structure, Reggie motioned Simone to follow him toward the encrusted belly of the ship. Simone could see the eyes of hundreds of curious fish watching them as they descended, and for the first time she felt a shiver of apprehension. Reggie pointed to a small area that he thought might be the ship's cabin and indicated to Simone that he wanted to take a look inside. Simone nodded and watched her diving companion wiggle his way through a narrow opening. The silt stirred up by Reggie's flippers made it difficult for her to see what was happening, so she waited patiently for things to settle down before moving closer.

When the water cleared, she peered inside the cabin and tried to see what Reggie was up to. To Simone's surprise, Reggie had disappeared. *Where is he,* Simone thought to herself as panic began to set in. When she stuck her head further into the narrow entranceway, she was greeted by the head of the goliath grouper. Jerking her body back, she scraped it against the top of the passageway and blood began to ooze from the wound. Rubbing the top of her head, she realized she had cut herself more than she thought and became concerned her blood might attract one of the sharks circling the area. Now, more than ever, she needed to find Reggie. Swimming to the top of the structure, she peered into an open passageway and tried to find him. He wasn't there. Turning around, she spotted a couple of bull sharks moving in her direction. Anxious about the sharks' intent, she quickly swam over to the next opening in the ship and looked inside—still no Reggie. *Where is he?* Now the sharks were moving closer. *Will they attack? They might decide to do so at any moment.* She knew these marine animals could be unpredictable, so rather than risk any more time looking for Reggie, she decided to swim up toward the boat and prayed she could make it to the surface before the sharks decided to attack. She was about halfway there when something grabbed hold of her leg and pulled her backwards. Certain it was one of the sharks, she jerked her leg and managed to pull herself free. In desperation, she raced to the surface, thankful not to see any blood oozing from her leg but too terrified to look back. "Help me," she cried out when she reached the stern of the boat and removed her mouthpiece.

"What's the matter?" Wendell asked as he reached over the side of the boat and helped Simone climb the ladder.

"Sharks," Simone panted as she looked down at her leg. "I'm certain one of them grabbed me."

"You look fine to me," Wendell assured her. "I don't see any bite marks."

Puzzled, Simone reached down and checked her flippers to see if perhaps a shark had grabbed hold of one of them, but there were no bite marks on either one. "I can't understand it. I was certain one of them attacked me."

"Can someone give a hand?" Reggie shouted.

"Coming," Wendell said. Bending over the boat's ladder, he took Reggie's flippers and face mask and helped him on board.

"What's de matter wid her?" Reggie asked when he observed Simone lying on the deck.

"She thinks she was attacked by a shark. She said one of them grabbed her when she was trying to swim to the surface."

"Dat wasn't any shark," Reggie laughed. "Dat was me. I grabbed her leg ta get her attention. I wanted ta show her something I found in de wreck."

Looking over at Reggie, Simone's anguish turned into anger. Embarrassed that she'd panicked and looked like a fool, she began yelling at Reggie for scaring the heck out of her. "You took off and left me alone down there. I thought something bad had happened, so I tried to find out if you were trapped in the wreck or one of those giant fish had tried to eat you for dinner. In the process, I scraped my head on the top of the ship's cabin. Then some sharks started to swim toward me. I was sure they were attracted by my blood and I had no choice but to leave you and head to the surface. Instead of grabbing hold of my leg, why didn't you swim up alongside and motion to me?"

"I'm sorry. I guess I should have. I didn't mean ta frighten you. I got so excited by what I discovered dat I wanted you ta swim down and see it."

"What did you find that made you so excited?" Wendell asked.

"Dis." Opening his gloved hand, Reggie showed them three gold coins. "Der's a whole cabin full of gold! Der're gold bars, silver and gold coins, and even jewelry with precious stones. We're rich beyond belief! Now I can buy de land on Fortune Island where my parents wanted to build der new home. Simone's father can build a bigger home fer her family, and maybe we can even buy our own boat and hire a captain and crew to take care of it when our families are taking vacations in different parts of de world."

Wendell stared with amazement at the coins and shook his head. Simone's reaction was different. As Wendell fondled the coins, her eyes welled up with tears and she began to cry.

"What's de matter?" Reggie asked. "Aren't you happy?"

"Shouldn't we also be using some of the money to help the less fortunate?" Simone interjected. "Like the people in Haiti who have just experienced horrific damage from an earthquake. All you think about is how rich we will become and all the things we can buy, but all I can think about is all the poor people in my homeland of Haiti and how much they are suffering. If we are going to become as rich as you say, we need to think about how we can share some of our new found wealth with other people so they can have better lives."

"You're right," Wendell admitted. "There are lots of ways we could use the treasure to help people build new schools and homes and find ways to get clean water to their communities. The list is endless. If we decide to use some of the money in this way, we'll need someone who can tell us the wisest path to follow. Your father is a smart man, I'm sure he will be able to help us."

"Well, we won't be able ta help anybody if we don't start collecting de treasure and begin hauling it up ta de cave. I'm afraid if someone else sees what we're up ta dey might start taking de treasure fer themselves."

"I agree," Wendell acknowledged. "But first we need to treat the cut on Simone's head so the blood oozing from it won't attract any sharks."

Hauling Treasure to the Cave

After Simone's head wound was treated, she and Reggie dove back to the wreck to retrieve more treasure.

Exhausted and panting, Reggie and Simone brought several more gold ingots to the surface and handed them to Wendell. Lifting off their face masks and mouth pieces, they grabbed hold of the boat's ladder and took a moment to rest. "These gold bars sure are heavy," Wendell grunted as he hauled in the last lot and placed it on the deck with the other valuable finds that his friends had brought to the surface. "How much gold and silver is left?" he asked.

"A lot more dan we can bring up taday," Reggie replied. "We need ta head toward de cave as soon as possible otherwise it'll be dark before we make it back ta Landrail. Give us a hand into de boat so we can take dis gear off and head back ta shore."

With their diving gear removed and stowed safely below, Reggie started the boat's engine and headed toward the cave site on Fortune Island.

"What was it like down there?" Wendell asked Simone as Reggie guided the boat south and moved it closer to the beach.

"It's creepy. The treasure is stored in a dark cabin that's still guarded by a giant goliath grouper. He doesn't attack or anything; he just watches us. Every time I swim past him, I wonder what it would be like if it grabbed hold of one of us. I swear to God, he's got a mouth so big he could gulp us down with one bite. Fortunately, he's never expressed any interest in attacking. I'm glad Reggie brought his spear gun for protection and I'm also glad we had underwater flashlights so we could see around the cabin. Even with them, it's difficult to make things out. There's so much sediment stirred up when we swim into the enclosure we have to wait a bit and let things settle before we collect the treasure and head back to the surface. The spookiest thing of all is the two skeletons we uncovered."

"Skeletons?!!" Wendell shrieked.

"Yes. One had a gold ring on its finger with a skull and crossbones made of ivory. Reggie insisted on removing it even though I shook my head and waved my hand telling him not to take it. I wanted him to leave it where it was; it gave me the creeps. When he pried the ring free, the skeleton's hand fell off and landed on the chest of jewels. The hand falling on the chest felt like a bad omen. I got the feeling it was warning us to leave the treasure where it was. When Reggie offered me the ring. I waved my hand again and indicated "no," but he just shrugged his shoulders and tossed it in with the rest of the treasure we'd collected. Besides the ring, we also found a round gold locket attached to a gold chain. The locket had a strange voodoo marking on its surface. If we can pry it open, I'd like to look inside before we put it with the rest of the treasure we collected."

"I remember seeing that locket," Wendell said. "It was in one of the mesh bags that Reggie gave me. Would you like me to get it now so you could study it more closely?"

"Sure, that would be great."

"Ok," Wendell said and stepped into the boat's cabin to get the mesh bag that contained the gold locket.

"What are you doing?" Reggie asked.

"I'm retrieving the locket you discovered. Simone wants to take a closer look at it."

"I'd like ta look at it ta, but let's do it after I move de boat closer ta de shore where de cave is located."

"Sure." Wendell nodded in agreement, walked to the bow of the boat and waited for Reggie to give him the sign he was ready for Wendell to cast the anchor overboard.

After Reggie turned the boat's bow into the waves, he yelled to Wendell to heave the anchor over the side. When the anchor's flukes grabbed some rocks, Wendell gave Reggie the thumbs up and the boat's stern swung toward the beach.

"Now de work begins," Reggie said.

"Before we start to unload the gold and jewels, I'd like to take a few moments to study this locket you collected," Simone told Reggie.

"What's so special about it?"

'There's a unique voodoo image carved on its surface. It's a skull and crossbones like the ones you see on the flag of a pirate ship. I've also seen this image before in one of the books they had at the university. When I read about its meaning in voodoo culture, it gave me an uneasy feeling. Do you think you could pry open this locket so we can see what's inside"?

"Maybe," Reggie responded. "But I'll have ta be very careful. De slightest mistake could cause dis locket ta break."

"I understand, but I really want to see what it conceals."

"All right. I have a small knife dat I can use ta scrape away some of de marine life growing over de outside. Once I do dat, I'll use de point of de blade to pry open de locket along its seam.

"Great," Simone responded with relief.

Scraping away the encrusted marine life took more time than Reggie had anticipated and he began to worry that this project wouldn't leave enough time to haul the rest of the treasure they'd collected to the cave before dark. Once the outside was completely cleaned, he used the blade's point to slowly pry open the locket. He then placed it into the palm of his hand, so he could show the inside to Simone.

Looking closely at what Reggie uncovered, Simone stepped back and gasped In horror.

"What's the matter?" Wendell said with concern.

"It-it's horrible" Simone stammered. "Close the locket and hide it some place. I never want to see it again."

Reggie gave Simone a strange look and gently closed the locket and put it in a plastic container he'd brought along for small pieces of treasure they had collected from the wreck.

"What did you see?" Reggie asked after putting away the sealed container with the rest of the treasure stored in the boat's cabin.

Tears rolled down Simone's face, as Wendell and Reggie waited for their friend to get control of herself and tell them what she saw.

"The locket is evil," she sobbed. "Just plain evil. What's in the locket isn't intended to bring health and happiness to someone; it's meant to bring harm. It contains what I'd guess to be the remains of human fingernails and hair collected from the body of a dead person. I was told by some people that lived in Haiti that the priests that own this type of locket belonged to a secret society. They said the locket gave them magical powers that enabled the priests to turn themselves into dogs and wild animals that would roam the villages at night where they could hunt down people they wanted to harm. The local Indians who knew about these priests called them skin walkers."

"You don't believe any of dat stuff?" Reggie laughed.

"Not initially," Simone sighed. "But when I saw what was in the locket, I'm not sure any more."

Holding on to the amulet that Simone had given him for protection, Wendell thought again about Japapa and was glad to know the evil priest had met his demise. Directing his friends' attention to the treasure they had collected, he reminded them that they needed to move the gold and jewels from the boat to the cave before it got dark.

"You're right," Reggie said. "We better get going."

Reaching down, Reggie picked up one of the gold bars and passed it to Simone. "Place it into one of de mesh bags I brought. We'll each carry one bag at a time ta de cave. It's ta heavy ta carry more gold dan dat."

The plan was that they would stack the gold in their hiding place and return to get some more. Since Simone still wouldn't enter the cave because of the bats, it would be her job to remain outside the cave to keep watch while Reggie and Wendell did the climbing and heavy lifting once they got inside the cave. It was exhausting work and they often had to stop and rest. After placing the gold bars in their hiding place, they went back to the boat and brought several sacks of gold coins and jewelry and hid them amongst the rest of the treasure.

"It's getting close to dark," Simone noted as the boys exited from the cave after dropping off the last lot. "We should head back to Landrail; otherwise, your uncle will begin to worry about us."

"How much longer do you think it will take to empty the ship of its treasure?" Wendell asked as the trio trudged back to the boat.

"Less dan a week," Reggie panted as they waded out to the boat. "Why?"

"Sharkman said there's a hurricane headed this way and that it's due to arrive sometime near the end of this week. He's moving his boat into a narrow mangrove creek where it will be safe from the storm. He's also taking shelter in the cave where Japapa held Simone captive. It appears if we're going to get the rest of this treasure removed from the ship and into the cave, we need to get it done before it arrives."

"I know all about dat storm. My uncle told me about it. He plans ta take his boat out fishing tomorrow wid his friends, but after dat he said we could have his boat until Saturday. When we finish using it, he's taking it up inta de mangroves to secure it der until after de storm passes. I'll make sure we're done by Friday. Dese storms never move in de direction de weather people say dey will, so I wouldn't get ta uptight about it until we know exactly where it's headed."

"You might be right about the storm, but I certainly don't want to get stuck out here in a hurricane," Wendell replied

"Neither do I," Simone concurred.

It was late afternoon on Friday by the time the youngsters removed nearly all the day's treasures from the sunken ship and moved it into the cave. All three were exhausted when they left the cave and made their way back to the beach. Looking up into the sky, they soon realized they'd never be able to make it to Landrail before the storm struck. The hurricane was arriving earlier than the weatherman predicted. Dark clouds were already swirling above their heads and the windblown water between Fortune Island and Landrail had been turned into a frothy maelstrom. Seven to ten-foot wind-generated waves were now racing northward and the trees and other vegetation near the shore of Fortune Island were being uprooted and carried down the beach.

"I knew we should have left sooner," Wendell grumbled as the trio headed back to the cave for shelter. Stinging sheets of rain and sand scoured their faces as they staggered back, while bolts of lightning splintered nearby trees and lit up the dismal layer of black clouds that blanketed the sky.

"I don't think there'll be much left of your uncle's boat by the time this storm passes," Wendell muttered.

"I knew I could depend on you ta tell me something I already know," Reggie snorted. "If we expect ta survive dis storm we need ta get away from de entrance of dis cave and move inside ta a safer place."

"And just where do you suggest we go?" Wendell retorted.

"De only place I can think of is de place where we hid de treasure. It's high enough up so dat we won't be swept away by any coastal flooding dat washes inta de cave."

"And what about me? Going back into that cave gives me the creeps." Simone shivered and scrunched up her face.

"Well, if you have a better idea I'm all ears, but you better tell me soon or we'll all be toast," Reggie replied.

"I don't," Simone sighed.

"Good. Den let's get going. We don't have much time."

Perfect, Baka thought to himself. *Everything is working just like I planned. Soon Sharkman and the teens will be swept up into my tangled web of destruction.* All of them had taken refuge in one of the caves just like he planned where total darkness would soon swallow them up and cast them into worlds beyond their imaginations. The success of his plan was exhilarating. He watched the hurricane he created grow stronger and bear down on his victims in the caves.

It is interesting that the youngsters found the gold locket. It is something that might prove to be very useful in my future plans. Right now, however, I have to deal with Mama Atabei.

The storm he had created had just passed over the island of Haiti. Many of the island's houses had been destroyed and criminals were tearing through the rubble looking for possessions they could exchange for food and money. *The islanders will soon need the priestess's help. Once the old woman becomes entangled with the job of trying to save them, she won't have time to rescue the youngsters and the old fisherman.*

Taking Shelter from the Storm

In all the years he lived in the Bahamas, Sharkman had never experienced a storm like this one. Taking refuge in the darkest recesses of the cave once occupied by Japapa, he listened in awe as the wind howled outside the entrance and bolts of lightning streaked across the ground, turning the sand into glass. Even the walls of the cave seemed to be shaking as the intensity of the hurricane increased. Had the youngsters made it back to Landrail safely? He hoped they had. There was no way Reggie's uncle's boat could survive the waves generated by this storm.

A strange sensation crept into the old man's thoughts as he sat scrunched up in the corner of the cave, arms folded over his knees. It was a feeling of dread. He couldn't quite put his finger on why he had this feeling but he was sure his life and the lives of the teenagers were in danger. As the storm raged on, he sensed someone or something evil was in the cave with him. He called out several times but there was no response. He continued to stare into the cave's darkest recesses as the caustic odor of burning sulfur and rotting flesh seeped into his nostrils. Once again, he called out and once again there was no response. He was sure he heard something moving around but he wasn't sure where. He listened carefully and thought he could just make out faint laughter when all of a sudden, he was sucked up into a dense vortex of darkness and flung toward a swirling ball of light.

"*You'll never forget this journey,*" Baka chuckled to himself. "*Planning your demise is giving me such pleasure. But before you die, I'll make sure you give me the location of the temple. Now, I must visit the other cave on Fortune Island. Your companions are waiting for me. They don't know I'm coming, of course, but they will soon experience a similar fate. Theirs, however, will be even worse than yours. They will be swept into the past to join up with a ruthless band of pirates.*"

As Baka's satanic presence faded from the cave, Sharkman's unconscious body was transported to a place no living person would want to go. Some would describe it as a living hell.

"I'm cold," Simone complained as she wrapped the rain slicker Reggie had grabbed from his uncle's boat. "I'm glad you thought to bring it."

"My only regret is that there weren't a couple more. How much longer do you think this storm will last?" Wendell asked Reggie.

"I haven't de faintest idea. Usually, dey pass through rather quickly, but dis one seems ta be hanging around forever."

"Well, I hope it's over soon," Simone interjected. "I can't imagine spending the night in this godforsaken place."

"It's not dat bad in here."

"Says who? The place stinks of bat guano and there must be a zillion cockroaches scurrying all over the place. They're running up my arms and legs and even getting entangled in my hair."

"Try ta ignore dem. Just make sure you keep your mouth shut. I'll have ta admit, dey don't taste very good."

"Thanks for the advice." Scrunching her face in disgust, Simone took her hand and swiped several of the insects away.

As the trio stared into the darkness, they anxiously listened to the storm's intensity increase. A river of water was now being driven into the cave and they soon could hear the water lapping at the rocks below their feet. "Are we high enough up so the water won't reach us?" Wendell asked.

"We should be," Reggie assured them.

"Oh my god!" Simone screamed and stood up.

Looking down at the rising wall of water with her flashlight, she stepped back and screamed as waves of cockroaches scrambled toward them. The roaches were like rats abandoning a sinking ship. Soon, everyone's body was covered in a blanket of bugs. In a desperate effort to rid themselves of the vile creatures, the trio dove into the rushing water and quickly discovered they couldn't swim against the raging current and were helplessly swept deeper into the cave. Soon they were transported into the darkest recesses until they found themselves being drawn toward a brilliant light at the end of a tunnel. The closer they got to the light, the brighter it became. Soon, they were blinded by its intensity. Shielding their eyes, they tried to see where they were headed but it was hopeless. A ferocious vortex in the current was about to hurl them into a world they would never forget.

Baka danced with glee as he watched the youngsters struggle to escape. No matter how they tried, they would not be able to free themselves. He couldn't think of anyone else except Sharkman who deserved a more horrible fate than this trio. But he intended to watch them closely to make sure everything went according to plan. Sharkman and the old priestess wouldn't be around to help them this time. The hurricane he had generated in Haiti would require all of the priestess's skills to save her people, while Sharkman would find himself hurled into a world that was soon to become buried in a layer of molten lava and volcanic ash.

Swept into the Past

When Sharkman regained consciousness, he saw two colorful, strange-looking fish staring at him. He would have liked to have spent a little more time staring back at them when he realized he couldn't breathe. Looking up, he spotted the water's sunlit surface and began swimming toward it. By the time his head bobbed above the ocean's surface, his lungs were about to burst. Turning around, he tried to determine where he was. In the distance, he spotted a large city with a Colosseum sitting on top of a hill. Beyond it towered a large volcano spewing ash and smoke into the air. There were also several small boats nearby. Maybe he could attract the attention of one of their crew. Waving and yelling, he started to swim in the direction of one of the larger boats. At first they didn't spot him. Then someone on board one of the vessels pointed in his direction and waved back. Several minutes later, one of their crewmen dragged Sharkman aboard their boat and began asking him all kinds of questions in a language he didn't understand. When he indicated he was a deaf-mute and motioned he needed something to write on, one of the crewmen found a piece of parchment and a writing tool. Sharkman wrote down his name, held the parchment against his chest, and pointed to himself. The crewmen just shook their heads and looked perplexed. It was obvious he had a serious communication problem. Pointing several more times to himself and the name he had written, he eventually got his rescuers to understand that Sharkman was his name.

For several minutes, the fishermen gathered amongst themselves and talked about the man they had just rescued, trying to decide what they would do with him. Finally, one of the crewmen wrote his name on a piece of parchment and placed it against his chest. The name he wrote was "Julius." Sharkman smiled and extended his hand to Julius to thank him. Nodding their heads, Julius and the crew returned his smile and welcomed him aboard their vessel. Sharkman then looked across the water, pointing toward the city he saw in the distance. Julius wrote on a piece of parchment the name "Pompeii" and held it up.

At that moment, reality set in and Sharkman stared at the city with concern. He had somehow traveled two thousand years into the past and was now staring at a city that had been destroyed by a volcanic eruption on the twenty-fourth of August 79 A.D. When the fishermen saw his face turn pale, they became concerned and encouraged him to sit down. At that point, Julius ordered a black crewman to give him some water. Sharkman sipped from a wooden ladle and tried to get his feelings under control.

What day and year is it? he wondered. *I'm not going to find out from these men, but somehow I need to know. I can't speak Latin and I'm not gifted in reading Roman numerals. It's evident I'm going to have to become a fast learner. This city I'm looking at is about to become obliterated by a volcanic eruption that will smother it in clouds of debris and ash. Few people will survive and two thousand years from now, archeologists will still be digging up the remains of the residents.*

While trying to develop an escape plan, he watched the men haul in a variety of fish. Some used handlines with squid for bait while others were very effective with cast nets. Their catch included several different species. The cast netters were bringing in mackerel and herring, while the hook and line fishermen brought up flounder, cod and sea perch. Watching them catch fish helped reduce his anxiety. If the fishermen didn't have other plans for him when they came ashore, he needed to figure out a way he could blend into the general population. The 20th Century clothes he was wearing were certainly not suitable in this time and place. He needed to acquire clothes that fit in with what other residents were wearing.

It was nearly sunset by the time the fishermen filled their hold with fish and headed back to shore. The crew seemed extremely happy with their catch and were topping off their successful day with jugs of wine. Sharkman accepted a jug from one of the crewmen, took several swigs, and then helped the crew sort the different kinds of fish. When the boat pulled into the harbor in the Saro River, one of the crewmen moored the bow of the boat to a ring along the rock wall and motioned to an elderly man with a beard. The man on shore quickly responded and brought them a dozen or so woven baskets for the fish. Sharkman helped the crew load the fish into the different baskets and hoist them ashore. When they were finished, the captain slapped Sharkman on the back and rewarded him with several *sestertius* and two fish for his assistance. The coins showed the bust of a Roman figure, which Sharkman later learned was Titus Flavius. Smiling, he bowed to the fisherman to thank him and wondered if the money he'd received was enough to trade for a new set of clothes. It was not, but the fish he'd been given turned out to be very valuable. He estimated each fish weighed about a pound and a half and later learned that each one was worth about 75 *denarius*. As he walked into town, he saw a shop with just the type of clothing he needed. Indicating to the shop owner he was a deaf-mute, he offered him a fish for some of the goods he had on sale. When the shop owner saw the fish in Sharkman's hands, he grinned from ear to ear and gave the fisherman a tunic, a simple loincloth and a pair of sandals in exchange for a fish.

After putting on his new attire, Sharkman ventured down one of the cobblestone side streets near the coast and looked for a market where he could buy something to eat. He hadn't eaten anything for a day and a half and wondered what kind of food he could get in exchange for his other fish. When he thought about his situation, he laughed to himself. *I can't imagine telling my friends back in Landrail there once was a time I hadn't eaten any food for nearly 2,000 years. None of them would believe me. They would accuse me of having too much to drink and suggest I go home and sleep it off.*

As he wandered further along through the streets of the city, he continued to think about the mess he was in. He had no idea how he was going to escape from this city before it was destroyed nor did he have any idea how he was going to return to his own time. He had little doubt that Baka was up to his old tricks, and this time it was going to be difficult for him to escape from the demon's clutches.

It was nearly dark when Sharkman found a shop near the waterfront that sold food. The shop owner seemed nervous when he approached but after showing him the fish the boat captain had given him, he said, "*Ubi tu furtum hoc* (Where did you steal this?)" Sharkman didn't have a clue what the shop owner had just said so he shook his head and indicated he couldn't hear or speak. The owner then gave the old man a suspicious look and grabbed the fish so he could study it. Satisfied that it was fresh, he reached into his pocket and offered Sharkman a half dozen silver coins. Pleased to get some additional money, Sharkman pointed to some stale bread and cheese on the counter. The proprietor nodded, handed him the food and took back one of the silver coins. Pleased with the transaction, Sharkman took the food and started to walk across the narrow street. "Wait!" the proprietor yelled, forgetting that the old man could not hear him. When he realized his mistake, the shop owner grabbed Sharkman by the shoulder and used his fingers to indicate it wasn't safe to be on the street at night.

At that point, Sharkman turned and gave the shop owner an odd look before realizing what he was trying to say. Pointing to a tenement building the owner said, "*Cubiculum.*"

Knocking on the door of the building manager, the shop owner told him that the fisherman needed a room for the night. "Why doesn't the old man ask for the room himself?" the manager replied when he opened his door.

"He can't hear or speak," the store proprietor told him. Once the manager understood, he agreed to provide Sharkman with an upstairs room that he thought the man would find comfortable.

"Does he have any money?" the building manager asked the shop owner.

"He does," and the shopkeeper motioned to Sharkman that the building manager wanted to be paid with one of the coins he'd given him. Sharkman reached into his pocket, gave him one and received several others in return.

The building manager then pointed at Sharkman and urged him to follow him up a series of worn, wooden stairs. Several flights up, he was shown a terrible smelling room that had a single wooden chair and table plus a straw bed that not even a goat would want to sleep in. Besides having no running water, the room also lacked a toilet. Sleeping here might be safer than being out on the streets overnight, but tomorrow, he was going to look for better accommodations. After the building manager left, Sharkman walked over to the straw bed and tried to arrange it so it would be more comfortable. He then stretched out and tried to think about how he could go about improving his living conditions. *Maybe the fisherman that had saved my life could help me. But whatever place I move into will only be a short term arrangement. Ultimately, I hope I can get one of the fishermen to take me to a place that is safer than Pompeii. If my gut feeling is correct, I don't have much time before this city will be buried in volcanic ash and almost everybody that lives here will die a horrible death.*

Tumbling down onto the beach, Reggie, Wendell and Simone slowly stood up, brushed themselves off, and stared at their new surroundings.

"Where are we?" Wendell asked.

"I haven't a clue," Reggie responded.

There was no longer any sign of the hurricane that had been pounding the island. A clear, cloudless sky stretched overhead and the wind-tossed ocean had been replaced by tranquil blue-green waters that stretched to the horizon. "Der should be lots of debris washed up on ta de beach and lots of trees knocked over by de storm but der is absolutely no evidence of dat."

"Yuk," Simone grumbled and began brushing away the cockroaches that still clung to her clothing. "The storm may have disappeared but a few of these roaches have managed to make the journey with us."

Ignoring Simone's distress over the insects, Reggie suggested they should start to explore the island. "If dis is Fortune Island, der should be a small community about a mile south of here. Maybe we can learn something from de people dat live der."

"Sounds like a good idea," Wendell said as he bent over to remove the last roach from Simone's pant leg.

"Thanks." Simone smiled. "I hate those things."

"That's obvious," Wendell laughed. Taking hold of Simone's hand, they followed Reggie down the beach to look for the small community at the end of the island.

After trudging south along the shoreline for an hour, they reached the end of the island and were dismayed when they found no evidence of the village Reggie expected to be there. He also hoped that they might locate his uncle's boat along the way, but apparently it had also vanished. "Dis is really weird," Reggie grumbled. "We should have come across de village. I think we should take a break and talk about things."

"I'm all for that," Simone agreed.

"Does anyone have a clue what happened ta us back der in de cave during de hurricane?" Reggie asked. "I've never experienced anything like dat and I've survived several severe storms on Crooked Island."

Simone and Wendell shook their heads. "What happened beats me," Wendell acknowledged.

"I only know it was the scariest thing I've ever been through in my short existence," Simone shuddered.

"I agree," Wendell said. "Do you think our old nemesis, the demon Baka had anything to do with it?"

"I wouldn't put it past him." Reggie responded. "Maybe he took possession of de gold locket we discovered and used its evil powers ta dump us off on dis abandoned island," he teased.

"I'm not so sure he discovered the locket. Nor do I feel he could use its powers to do what you suggest," Simone responded.

"Well, if it's not Baka, we could make our way back ta Landrail where I can get another boat. Once I do, I could use it ta look fer my uncle's vessel. If we can't find it, we should buy him another one wid de gold we've stored in de cave."

"That depends on whether or not the gold and artifacts are still in the cave or whether the cave is even there," Wendell replied. "Knowing Baka, there's a good chance they aren't. His plan would be more sinister than that."

"Like what?" Simone asked and gave Wendell a curious look.

"I know this sounds far-fetched, but suppose he sent us back in time," Wendell suggested.

"That is pretty far-fetched," Simone admitted. "But you could be right. The fact that we haven't found the village or our boat fits with that idea."

"There is no telling what he intends to do to get even with us," Wendell said. "He might plan to have drug smugglers capture us."

"It doesn't sound cruel enough ta me. If he's planning ta take his revenge out on us, it would have ta involve something dat includes pain and torture."

"You're probably right," Simone groaned. "That would probably make him very happy."

"Maybe he'll decide to slice us up and feed us to the sharks. That type of punishment seems to be high on his list," Wendell interjected.

"I think we'll know soon," Simone said as she stood up, shielded her eyes from the sun and looked across the water. "I think we have visitors."

"Where?" Reggie asked as he stood up alongside Simone. Looking across the water, he spotted the ship she was looking at. "I don't believe it," he groaned. "It's a pirate ship and dey are flying der Jolly Roger. I believe dey've just launched a boat and it's headed straight toward us."

"I guess we're about ta learn what Baka's plans for us are," Wendell added.

Grabbing Simone's hand, Reggie raced inland and yelled to Wendell to follow. He didn't need to give his friend any encouragement. He'd read enough about pirates to know they were in deep trouble. Hopefully, they'd find a safe place to hide until this band of buccaneers left.

"Over dere!" Reggie shouted and motioned to Wendell. "Hurry! crawl inta dos bushes."

"They're covered with thorns," Wendell complained. "Couldn't you find a better place for us to hide?"

"Dat's de whole idea. Dos pirates will never look fer us amongst dese thorny acacia trees."

"How do you know they even spotted us?" Simone asked as she struggled into the bushes and settled down next to Reggie. Looking at her torn clothing and the scratches on her arms, she frowned and hoped that this idea was worth all the trouble.

"Oh, dey spotted us all right. It is impossible fer dem not ta. Think about it. How difficult would it be fer you ta spot three black people standing on a white sand beach on a bright, sunny day?"

"You're right," Wendell admitted. "It would be pretty hard for them not to miss us."

"Now let's pray dey don't find us. Try not ta move and stay as quiet as you can," Reggie whispered.

"That's easy for you to say," Simone complained. "I've got sand flies crawling up my nose and chewing the rest of me to pieces. It feels like my skin is on fire."

"I know, but it's better dan being carted off ta Nassau ta be sold as slaves."

"He's right," Wendell conceded as he tried to endure the biting insects. "I've read about what happened to black children when pirates captured them and I'd much rather be here than aboard their ship."

Their hiding place became less and less tolerable as the day progressed. Sweat seeped into their open wounds making their skin burn even more, and it was impossible to keep the no-see-ums from crawling up their noses and into their eyes. The mosquitoes also became a problem. There were hordes of them sucking blood from every inch of their bodies. Although none of them wanted to admit it, they didn't know how much longer they could endure hiding in the bushes.

"Do you think they're gone?" Simone whispered. "We've been hiding in these bushes for nearly two hours and I can't stay here much longer."

"I agree," Wendell groaned. "I can hardly prevent myself from slapping at these blood sucking monsters."

"Let me check things out." Crawling out from under the bushes, Reggie stealthily made his way up to the top of a sand dune in front of the bushes and searched for signs of the pirates and their wooden jolly boat. After scanning the beach for several minutes, he crawled back into the bushes where Simone and Wendell were hiding, and announced, "As far as I can tell, de men have left. It's safe fer us ta come out."

"Thank god," Wendell sighed as he and Simone crawled out of the bushes and joined Reggie on an open patch of sand. By now, their eyelids were almost swollen shut and their faces were puffed up from mosquito bites. The rest of their exposed skin was scratched open and bleeding from the thorns on the acacia trees and their bodies were still burning from the no-see-ums that had burrowed into their skin.

"I think it's safe fer us ta head down ta de beach. A cool swim will soothe all dese bites and scratches," Reggie suggested.

"That's the best idea you've had all day," Wendell replied with an edge of sarcasm. Without another word, all three stripped down to their underwear, raced across the beach, and jumped into the cool, clear water surrounding Fortune Island.

"This is heavenly," Simone sighed as they floated on the surface and watched the sun begin to set in the west. "I wonder what happened to the pirates that were rowing ashore?"

"We're right behind you, Matey."

Jumping up and turning around, the three teens stared with their mouths agape. Four of the scruffiest human beings they'd ever encountered were staring back at them. Their faces were covered with thick beards, knitted red caps covered their heads, and the rest of their patchwork clothing consisted of grease-coated breeches and loose fitting shirts that didn't look like they'd been washed in years.

"So you landlubbers thought you'd get away from us by hiding in the bushes? Seems you were wrong."

Laughing, one of the pirates leered approvingly at Simone and grinned, "Our captain will really enjoy the company of a pretty, young wench like you. We'll chain the rest of you rapscallions below deck. On the other hand, maybe our captain will decide to let you help us with our work aboard ship until we reach New Providence. I'm sure, by then, he'll figure out what to do with you. I suspect you'll fetch a mighty good price at the slave market."

The scruffiest of the pirates then motioned to one of the others to bring their boat closer. "Tie their hands behind their backs and toss this lot into our jolly boat," he snarled. "The less they can move around, the less trouble they will be."

"Now we're in for it," Wendell grumbled as his hands were tied behind his back and he landed next to Reggie.

"Do you think you need ta tell me dat?" Reggie whispered while giving one of the pirates a look of defiance.

"Hey, Mates, these Africans speak some kind of strange English," one of the pirates shouted to the others after listening to Reggie and Wendell's conversation. "That could make them even more valuable when the captain goes to sell them at the slave market."

One of the other pirates laughed as he grabbed hold of the oars. "He might even give us an extra reward for capturing them."

"I agree. We could use the money to buy some more drafts of rum," another chuckled and slapped his crewmate on the back. "Let's get back to the ship and deliver our prizes."

The powerful, Haitian priestess, Mama Atabei, paused for a moment to survey the devastation that surrounded her in Haiti. It would take years for the destruction caused by the last earthquake and the recent hurricane for the city to be repaired. She would do everything she could to help her people return to normal, but there was something else tugging at her thoughts. She couldn't quite put her finger on what it was, but she suspected Baka had some role to play in the devastation she saw. *Was the demon responsible for the hurricane and the chaos and loss of life it had generated? If so, why? Was it to distract me from something else? If that's the case, what is he trying to distract me from? I think I know, but I don't have time to deal with it right now; there are too many other problems to solve.*

But soon—very soon, I will have to find out what this evil demon was up to.

The satanic Baka was delighted with his success. The old fisherman was stuck in a city that was about to be destroyed by a volcanic eruption, and the youths had been captured by a band of ruthless pirates. Pacing back and forth, he tried to think of ways he could make things even worse. *I need a quiet place to think, a place far away from the screams and moans of the evil people that have been sent to my underground kingdom to suffer for their sins.* As he sat upon his fiery throne, he conjured up a number of possibilities. *I need another person to help me with my plan. Who will be the best person to do it?* At that point, a delicious idea came to him. Jumping up, he returned to his burning cauldron of tortured souls and spotted just the individual he needed. Looking down, he saw him crawling around in the pit of boiling tar. *Yes! The voodoo priest, Japapa, is definitely the person to help me carry out my plan, and there is no doubt he will agree to help, especially when I offer him a second chance to spend the rest of his life away from the eternal fires of Hell.*

Fleeing the Storm

While Sharkman and the teens huddled in caves and were being swept into the past by Baka, the enormous hurricane raged in the Bahamas. Winds up to 150 mph slammed into Crooked Island and the surrounding areas. No one was prepared for the storm's fury and no one could believe how quickly it had arrived. Wendell's parents and his sister were still visiting his grandfather, Reggie's uncle had borrowed a friend's boat and was out fishing, and Claude Joseph was filling out forms for the school in his office. As the winds grew fiercer and the ocean began to surge across the low lying areas, people started rounding up their children and relatives and looking for some place where they could retreat to safety on higher ground. Claude Joseph and his family and Reggie's uncle knew where the youngsters were supposed to be but they had no time to rescue them. They could only hope that they would find a safe place to hide from the storm.

Two hours after the swirling edge of the hurricane hit, trees were uprooted, branches were hurled through the air like harpoons, and numerous roofs were torn from houses. Boats that had been anchored in mangrove creeks quickly filled with rising water and sank, while those anchored in the bays broke from their moorings and were smashed against the island's jagged lime rock shore. For many people, it was hard to find a place to go. Some huddled in boats tied to the wooden frames of their homes while others sought refuge in caves carved into hillsides. At one point, the sound of the storm whipping across the island became so loud people couldn't hear one another talk. All they could do was pray. No one was coming to rescue them any time soon and it would be a long time before any medical help reached the island to treat the injured.

Claude Joseph ran across the street to his house during the raging storm. He realized the best place to take shelter from the hurricane was for him and his family to lock themselves in their bathroom. Grabbing some blankets to protect them, Claude and his son leaned against the bathroom door while his wife huddled in the tub.

A surge of rising water swept through Wendell's grandfather's house and propelled the family through a broken window. In desperation, they grabbed the trunk of an Australian pine and were carried to an inland swamp. After the pine became entangled in a cluster of mangrove trees, they deserted their temporary life raft and searched for higher ground. Fortunately for them, there was a rocky outcropping about a quarter of a mile away from where their tree had become ensnared in the mangroves. Wading through waste deep water and thick mud, they made it to a rocky ledge before the receding water could suck them back into the ocean. Unfortunately, the relief they felt when they reached high ground was only momentary. When evening arrived, they were enveloped in a thick, black cloud of mosquitoes. The constant drone of their wings and the persistent bites of these blood-sucking insects made it impossible to sleep. After the storm clouds disappeared and the stars lit up the clear night sky, they could barely make out their surroundings through their swollen eye lids. *How long will we be able to survive out here*, Ben thought to himself as he looked over at the rest of his family. He was too exhausted to think about that now. Tomorrow they would make plans to return to Landrail and see if any rescue ships were on their way with food and water. He could only pray that Wendell was still alive, but there was nothing he could do to search for him and his friends until things had begun to return to normal.

Lewis Sands was out on a friend's boat he had borrowed to go fishing when he spotted the storm clouds of the hurricane approaching. He knew it was coming but hadn't expected it to arrive this soon. There was no time to waste. He stopped fishing, started up the boat's engine, and headed back to Landrail. He needed to get back to his wife and children before the storm struck the island. Thirty minutes from shore, lightening started striking all around him and the wind's intensity increased to about 40 miles per hour. It took all of his skill to plow through the wind generated waves and keep the boat headed toward shore. Just about the time he felt he was going to make it, the heavens opened up and sheets of blinding rain made it impossible for him to see. By keeping his eye on the boat's compass, he knew he was headed in the right direction. The problem was the abundant coral patch reefs that were present in the island's shallow waters. He couldn't see well enough to maneuver around them. Praying that he'd make it back without running into them, he pointed the boat's bow due east to avoid the treacherous reefs. It didn't work. Within minutes, the vessel struck one of the reefs and the boat began to sink.

As the waves swept over the sinking boat, he jumped into the storm-tossed water and started to swim toward shore. It didn't take long for his feet to touch bottom. Fighting the storm's waves, he wondered if he would make it to the beach. The answer was no. Large waves slapped into his back and catapulted him down the beach before he could reach the shore. Tumbling over in the waves, he was tossed onto a sandy beach where he was able to crawl to safety among the island's dunes. *How far away from my house am I?* Lewis asked himself. He had no idea. Perhaps if he stood up he could see his house. Another mistake. The minute he tried to stand, strong winds and sheets of rain slammed him back to the ground. The only way he was going to make it to his house was by trying to crawl his way inland. At times he didn't think he would make it. Wind driven sand scraped away his skin and broken, thorny branches of acacia trees tore his clothes. By the time he reached the front door of his house, his face was a bloody mess and the only clothes he had on were the tattered remnants of his undershirt and pants. Banging on the front door, he hoped his wife was still there and would hear his plea for help. She did. The door opened and Mrs. Sands pulled her battered husband to safety.

"We can't stay here," Lewis frantically said to his wife when she finished patching him up. "If we stay here, we'll all be killed. Is de car still working?"

"As far as I know," she replied.

"Good. Pack it with all de food and clothing we'll need fer a week. Den I'll drive us inland ta a place where we'll be protected from de wind and storm surge."

"You're in no condition ta drive. You tell me where you think de best place ta go is and I'll drive us der."

Lewis nodded in agreement and his wife and the children hurriedly loaded their supplies into the car and climbed into the vehicle. "Head toward de hills outside of town," Lewis shouted. "Der is a cave near an outcropping on de hill where we can take refuge."

As they drove out of Landrail, the children watched from the rear seat of the car as a gigantic wave rose up out of the ocean and smashed into their home.

"Papa, our house was just swallowed by de ocean," one of the children screamed.

"I'm not surprised," Lewis's wife sobbed and refused to look back at the destruction taking place. Things would not return to normal for a long time.

Pompeii

He'd slept on the hard deck of a boat and on rocky ground in a sleeping bag but nothing compared to trying to rest on a mat of lice-filled straw dumped on the wooden frame of a bed. He itched throughout the night and by morning, he was barely able to stand up. Stretching his aching body, he staggered to a poorly carved wooden table, sat on the room's only chair, and consumed a piece of stale bread and a slice of moldy cheese for breakfast. Both had been chewed on by rats, but it was better to share it with them than having nothing to eat. As the sun rose above the horizon, he listened to a rooster crow outside his room and began to think about a place where he could clean himself up. Then he remembered the fountain in the park near the fishing boats that he passed the previous night.

The water flowing in it looked cool, clean, and refreshing and might serve his purpose.

He gingerly made his way down a rickety flight of wooden steps that led out of his building. Once outside, he entered one of the most foul-smelling environments he'd ever encountered. As he headed down the cobblestone street, he wanted to vomit. Then someone suddenly yelled from above, "Videte! (look out!)," and cast a bucket of human waste in front of him. The street was covered with human and animal scat that had attracted an enormous population of flies. He held his nose to block out the stench and quickly made his way toward the crowded fountain in the park. When he got there, people were washing themselves and scrubbing their clothes in the clear water collecting at the bottom. After drinking some of the fresh water bubbling from the top to wash away the moldy taste of his breakfast, he removed his clothes and joined the rest of the naked people who were washing their clothes at the base of the fountain. When he was finished cleaning his clothes, he wrung them out and prepared to lay them in a sunny place to dry when the ground began to shake and the water in the fountain stopped flowing. Others who had come to the fountain to clean themselves looked up at the volcano in fear and began running toward the pier. Bricks from the apartment buildings started tumbling into the street and stray dogs wandering through the city with their tails tucked between their legs began to howl.

Was this the day the city of Pompeii would be destroyed? The history books he had read had mentioned earthquakes taking place prior to the eruption of the volcano. Putting on his wet tunic and loincloth, Sharkman quickly joined the other terrified citizens racing toward the water's edge. To everyone's relief, the ground beneath their feet stopped shaking shortly after they reached the boat docks and things quickly appeared to return to normal. When he turned around and looked back up at the volcano, he was glad to see that the large amounts of ash and debris that it had been spewing from its caldera the previous day had stopped and everyone had begun looking around at each other with a sigh of relief. The residents of Pompeii had survived another day. Unlike the earthquake that had taken place sixteen years earlier and killed some 2,000 people, this one was mild and seemed to have caused little damage. Gratified nothing serious was about to happen, the local citizens wandered back into the city and started to conduct their daily routines hoping that there would not be another event.

"*Grata* (Welcome)," someone from behind Sharkman said and placed their hand on the old man's shoulder. Turning around, Sharkman was greeted by the smiling face of the fisherman who had saved his life the previous day. Acknowledging the greeting with a nod of his head, he reached out, clutched the captain's shoulder, and smiled.

"*Sequi* me. (Follow me.)" The captain waved his hand and motioned Sharkman to follow. When they got to his boat, he pointed to some damaged nets on the vessel's bow, picked one up, and indicated that he wanted them repaired. Sharkman nodded, then showed with his hands that he would need a device to mend them. The captain returned with the needle needed to repair the nets, took the fisherman's hand and invited him aboard. Smiling, Sharkman sat down on the deck and began threading together the torn pieces of fishing nets.

"*Gratias tibi.* (Thank you.)" The captain grinned and left the old man to his work.

Thinking about the events that just had happened, Sharkman once again thought about his future. *Perhaps there is a way to escape from this city after all. From the earthquake I just experienced, I know it won't be long before the city will undergo another event and be buried in ash and lava. It won't take place for a while, if I'm lucky. By then, I might be able to convince the man I am working for to drop me off at a place far away from the city. The question is where do I want to go and how can I get the man to take me there?*

A few days later, there was strong wind blowing across the offshore waters of Pompeii and the bay had been stirred into a frothy tempest. No one would be going out fishing today. Sharkman realized that meant he would have extra time to repair the nets. But he would need a few more of the needle-like devices the captain had given him to do the repairs. His first stop would be the warehouse nearby. It stored all types of fishing equipment and he would need quite a bit of it to repair the nets waiting for him. He had gotten the money to buy the goods he needed from the captain and was delighted to see that the warehouse was open at six in the morning. Walking through the building, he picked up different size needles and twines as well as a variety of floats and weights. It didn't take him too long to select what he wanted, and after paying the owner for the supplies, he headed down to the boats to begin his task.

He had been lucky. During the past few days, the local fishermen found his skills very useful and he was being paid extremely well for his knowledge as a fisherman and his abilities to repair nets and boats. As he approached the pile of damaged nets, Antonio walked up to him and offered to help. The young man was the son of the captain who had pulled him out of the ocean and saved his life, and during the last few days, he and Sharkman had become friends and Antonio had been trying to teach the old man Latin while he was working on the nets.

Sharkman was happy for him to help. Sitting together on two wooden barrels, they assessed the damage to the nets. Those with holes that were too big were set aside to be repaired later. Those with smaller holes, missing floats and weights were placed in a second pile to be worked on immediately. When the initial sorting process was complete, Sharkman picked up one of the nets with smaller holes and placed it over his knee. Reaching into his satchel, the old man pulled out several pieces of mending twine and two fish-netting needles. He gave some twine and a needle to the boy; the rest he saved for himself. At this point, Sharkman wrapped about 12 inches of twine around the needle then spread the net out flat across his lap to look for holes. When he found one, he connected the torn mesh with the twine and on the last stitch, he passed the needle inside the loop he created and pulled on the twine to tighten the knot.

The young man followed by selecting another net with a hole in it and very carefully replicated the procedure Sharkman had used to repair his net. Proudly lifting up the repaired section of net when he had finished, Antonio showed it to the old man with a smile. Sharkman examined the net and gave him two thumbs up. Working together, they finished all their net repairs by noon and agreed it was time to relax and have some lunch. Bread and cheese were on the menu.

After lunch, Sharkman decided he needed another lesson in Latin. Rolling out a piece of parchment, the old man drew an object and wrote down its English name. Antonio then wrote down its Latin equivalent. Some of the first words Sharkman learned were *piscatorum navibus* (fishing boats), *piscandi retia* (fishing nets), *domum* (home), and the phrase *iter ad domum* (travel to home). The boy then wrote on the parchment "*Visne domum ire?* (Do you want to go home?)" and wondered if the old man understood what he had written. Sharkman stared quizzically at the Latin words the boy had written. He scrunched his shoulders and raised the palms of his hands into the air to suggest he didn't understand what the boy was attempting to say. Trying to ask his question in a different way, Antonio drew a picture on the parchment to show what he meant. The old man's face grew sad. There was no doubt that he knew what Antonio had drawn on the parchment. He lifted his head and wistfully stared out across the water. Then he turned toward the boy and nodded yes. Antonio replied by picking up the quill pen lying next to them and began writing "*Tu me tecum?* (Will you take me with you?)" and drawing a picture of what he meant. Sharkman shook his head no. Disappointed by the old man's response, Antonio wiped a tear from his cheek and slowly stood up and walked back to his father's boat.

It's hard to say no to the boy, Sharkman thought. *I owe him a lot.* Through his efforts, he learned about the Latin calendar and realized that the eruption of Vesuvius was going to take place about a month from now. That would give him time to arrange his passage across the Bay of Naples to the island of Capri. But leaving the young man behind meant Antonio and his father would experience a sudden and horrible death. He just couldn't come to grips with that. On the one hand, he knew the boy's father loved his son dearly and was happy to see him learning more about the fishing trade from Sharkman. He also was aware that since the boy's mother died, his father wanted the boy to stay in Pompeii and raise a family. Sharkman thought a lot about this dilemma, especially at night when he went home. *Perhaps I could save them both. I've earned enough money to book passage for each of them. I could concoct some kind of story that would entice them to visit Capri before the volcano erupts.* The question was just what kind of story could be created that would it be convincing enough to get them to leave.

81

Pirate Ship–
Meeting an Old Acquaintance

Forcing Reggie, Wendell, and Simone to stand up in the jolly boat, as the pirates pulled it alongside the ship, one of the crew told his mates to untie their hands. He then shoved the youngsters toward the ship's ladder and ordered them to climb aboard. "The ship's a real beauty, don't you think?" one of the pirates said to the trio of mates and laughed. "Our captain captured her off the Florida Keys. She was loaded with lots of gold and silver and all kinds of precious jewels. I guess the king of Spain will miss out being able to use this booty to build his new fleet."

Once the teens climbed the ladder and boarded the ship, they took a moment to look around and rub away the pain in their wrists. "What do you think they will do with us?" Wendell asked Reggie.

"I don't know, but I can promise you it will not be anything good," Reggie said and shook his head.

"What's the name of your captain?" Simone asked.

"Black Caesar. Perhaps you've heard of him."

"I don't think I have," Simone replied.

"Well, he seems to know a lot about the three of you. He told us your names before he requested that you be picked up."

With a quizzical look, Reggie whispered in Simone's ear, "What did he just say?"

"Only his name and the fact that he seems to know a lot about us. They call him Black Caesar."

Reggie then turned to Wendell and asked, "Have you read anything about a pirate called Black Caesar?" Before Wendell could answer, one of the pirates told them to shut up and he shoved them toward the cabin at the stern of the ship. Knocking on the captain's door, the pirate announced their arrival.

"Welcome," the captain responded in a gruff voice.

After pushing the youths into the foul-smelling room, the crewman left and closed the cabin door. Black Caesar's back was to them while he scanned the shoreline of Fortune Island through the ship's rear windows. "It's a beautiful island, don't you think? I often wondered what it would be like to live here."

Turning around, the captain smiled. Black Caesar's six-foot-two height, muscular body and his friendly demeanor gave hope to the youths that their situation might not be as bad as they initially thought. Perhaps they would be able to convince him not to sell them as slaves.

"It's so nice to meet up with old friends again—don't you agree?"

Reggie and Wendell were stunned by the pirate's comment. "I don't think we've met you before, sir," Reggie stammered. "You must have us confused wid someone else."

"We've crossed paths before. On Castle Island. Of course, I didn't look like this. Baka has let me take possession of Black Caesar's body," Japapa laughed. "It's certainly more appealing than the last one I had, don't you think?"

Reggie's and Wendell's eyes and mouths opened wide in disbelief, and they began to tremble. Meanwhile, Simone's knees buckled and she blurted out, "You!" before she collapsed onto the deck in shock.

"Your companion seems to have fainted and needs something to revive her. I know how you must feel right now, but I'm sure you'll appreciate the arrangements I've made on your behalf."

Looking through the drawers in the ship's cabin, the captain eventually found a small brown bottle and gave it to Reggie. "It's smelling salts. It won't hurt your friend," the captain chuckled. "Just wave it under her nose. It will revive her. It's worked on others I've used it on."

Still trembling, Reggie knelt on the deck and waved the smelling salts under Simone's nose. After a couple of whiffs, she pushed the bottle away with her hand, lifted her head and groaned.

"I'm glad to see you've rejoined our little gathering," the captain said. "Still a beautiful young wench. What a magnificent wife you would have made me. Alas, my plans for you have changed. Different times, different solutions. Although I have to admit, having Claude Joseph's daughter married to a powerful voodoo priest like myself would have been a masterful stroke. With you at my side as my wife, there is absolutely no doubt I would have become Haiti's most powerful leader. But now there is no need for me to do that.

"I'm much better off being the captain of a pirate ship. No one here cares about drugs. The crew has plenty of rum to drink and there are more fortunes to be made capturing Spanish ships laden with a booty of gold and jewels. I'm already a very rich man and soon I'll become even richer. Ultimately, I plan to form a partnership with my good friend, Blackbeard. He seems to be as excited about the idea as I am.

"And you, Wendell, my little sniveler. What do you have to say for yourself?"

Unable to stop trembling, Wendell found it difficult to stand when he tried to answer. "W-we thought you were dead," he stammered. "You drowned. We saw you and your boat and most of your drug-smuggling followers sucked into a whirlpool off Castle Island and dragged to the bottom."

"Do I look dead to you?" the captain chuckled. "I must admit that your escape created a lot of problems for me. When my crew reported back that they had captured you, I was overjoyed. It's too bad I didn't succeed in slitting your throat, drinking your blood, and casting you into the fire as a sacrifice to Baka when I had the chance. My failure made Baka very angry. He saved me from drowning, but cast me and the rest of my gang into a fiery cauldron of hot tar in Hell. It was not the most ideal environment. As you can imagine, it was an extremely painful experience. When Baka saw the opportunity to get revenge on the three of you, he retrieved me from that hideous pit and offered me a second chance. He placed me into the body of the pirate Black Caesar, while you were being swept back in time. He demanded I take out his revenge on you. Of course, I was delighted to do that. The thought of meeting up with the three of you again gave me such a warm feeling inside."

"But your crew must know that you're not Black Caesar," Wendell stammered.

Stepping in front of Wendell, the pirate grinned. "How very insightful. However, only you and your friends know me as the voodoo priest Japapa. The rest of the crew sees me as their captain, Black Caesar."

"Very clever," Reggie snorted with disgust.

"I thought you would think so," Japapa acknowledged. "I must admit that I was sorry about having to kill your parents. It apparently was totally unnecessary, but when they decided to build their home on Fortune Island, I was afraid they might interfere with my drug-smuggling operation. As things turned out, they wouldn't have been a problem," the priest admitted.

Clamping his fists in a fit of rage, Reggie glared at Japapa with a feeling of contempt. If he had some way to kill the priest he would.

"And Sharkman. What did you do ta him?" Reggie asked as he glared at the voodoo priest.

"Ah yes, Sharkman. That old fool is more trouble than he is worth," Japapa smirked. "He's been transported back to the time of the Roman Empire, when the city of Pompeii still existed. I'm sure he'll enjoy being smothered under a cloud of volcanic ash. I understand from Baka that is a terrible way to die. Too bad the three of you won't be there to watch it happen."

"How thoughtful of you," Reggie growled. "So what do you intend ta do wid us?"

"Good question. You have been a problem ever since we encountered one another. First, I'll get Wendell and you some appropriate rags to wear and then I'll have my crew take you to the forward hold of the ship where you'll be chained together with some of my other captives. Unfortunately, you won't be able to converse much with them since most of them are Spaniards. These captives aren't much use to me, but they might have some entertainment value to the crew. I might have some of them walk the plank into shark-infested waters. Baka thought my crew would really enjoy seeing them get devoured by these creatures. The rest I'll probably abandon on one of the small uninhabited islands near here. Without any food or water, they won't last very long. As for you two, I'm thinking about selling you in the slave market in Nassau. There are always English patriots looking for strong young men to work their plantations. I'm sure they'll find you to be extremely useful. Or I could sell you to the men that operate the salt mines in Bonaire. The work there is a lot more grueling and

I don't expect either one of you would live very long in that environment."

"And what about Simone?" a distraught Wendell asked.

Lifting Wendell's chin up so he could look into his eyes. Japapa nodded and said, "I see you have feelings for the young lady. I regret to say you won't be spending too much time with her especially since you may be working in the salt mines.

"As for you, Simone, I'm not sure what I will do with you. I could hand you over to the men on my ship. I'm sure they would be happy to have you join them until we reach New Providence. On the other hand, I might get more fun out of selling you at the slave market. There are always colonists coming to the Bahamas who are looking for house maids, especially ones that speak both English and French. For now, I have a lot of work for you to do. After I get you some new clothing, I think I'll have you swab the deck of my cabin, prepare meals for me and clean up the mess my crew makes. I'm sure I'll also find some other delightful chores for you."

Stepping outside his cabin, Japapa motioned two of his men inside and ordered them to get Wendell and Reggie some new clothes, take them below deck, and chain them to the other prisoners. "The young lady will be staying with me," Japapa chuckled as his two crewman left with their prisoners. Both men nodded and smiled to one another as they left. By the grin on their captain's face, they were certain he would have an enjoyable evening with his new wench.

Haiti–Mama Atabei

In the 15th century, Haiti had initially been inhabited by native Indian tribes known as the Arawaks and Caribs. Christopher Columbus discovered the island in 1492 and promptly claimed the land for the Spanish Crown. When the Spanish were in control of the island, almost the entire Indian population of nearly 600,000 was wiped out. Most believed this happened because of diseases introduced by the Europeans. In 1697, possession of the island was placed under the control of two European countries. France occupied the western half and Spain the eastern portion. The western side of the island was eventually given the name Haiti, and Haitian Creole emerged as the language of the country.

During the French occupation, slaves from Africa were brought to the island to work the coffee and sugar cane plantations resulting in Haiti becoming one of the wealthiest of all New World colonies. As lore would have it, the African people summoned the evil demon, Baka, from Hell to help defeat their French slave owners. In 1771, the African slaves revolted against the French and in 1804, they established the first black republic. Many different leaders had taken control of the country since that time. Some of them were good; others were not.

The evil ones left an indelible mark on the Caribbean nation. Some of them were cruel people, like the voodoo priest Japapa, who worked for despicable leaders. These men tortured and killed many of their own people to satisfy their greed and lust for power. When Mama Atabei and Claude Joseph successfully revolted against Japapa and drove their last president out of the country, she had hoped more honorable people would take over their government and that life on the island would improve significantly. For a while, it did. But after the earthquake, things were once again in turmoil.

As Mama Atabie reflected about her country's history, she tried to think of a solution to the island's problems. *It would be good if a man like Simone's father could take over leadership of the country. He had a good education, was honest, knew a lot about the country's constitution, and if he was the island's leader, she felt certain he would do everything in his power to make the lives of the people better. Would he be willing to do it? Perhaps, I'll talk to him about it when I return to Crooked*

Island. In the meantime, I will speak to some of my followers to find out what sinister plans Baka is attempting to carry out.

Pacing back and forth in the room Mama Atabie had rented in Port-au-Prince, the priestess was deeply saddened by the events she was observing since the recent hurricane. The price for fuel had risen out of sight, jobs were hard to find and very few people could afford food. Criminals were breaking into shops and stealing goods from homes. Only the well-to-do and the political elite were able to maintain comfortable life styles. Corruption was growing in the political ranks and living conditions for most of the people on the island had become worse. In addition, the island's residents suspected that their newly elected president was under the control of corrupt men. They included some of the island's military leaders as well as some business people who were profiting from the monetary aid that was being sent to the country after the recent hurricane. Things needed to change, but at the moment, Mama Atabei had no idea how that was going to become a reality.

The Haitian priestess had done her best to see that people's lives would be returned to normal. However, she was anticipating more riots would soon break out in the streets and she doubted the island's leadership had the will to suppress them.

She was also anxious to hear back from one of her followers about the fate of Sharkman and the youngsters on Crooked Island. She recently heard rumors that Crooked Island had been devastated by the hurricane and many of its residents were also in dire need of help. As she looked out the window at the people gathering in the streets, there was a loud knock at the door. "Who's there?" she asked.

"It's Samuel. I'm here to report what I found out about Sharkman and the youths on Crooked Island."

"Come in. The door is open."

"I'm sorry I took so long. It was difficult to get transportation to Port-au-Prince and the crowds gathering in the streets made it even harder for me to get into the hotel."

"I understand," Mama Atabei sighed. "What did you find out?"

"As you are aware, Crooked Island's residents are just recovering from the hurricane but I did get to speak to some of Reggie's friends. None of them has been in touch with the teens or Sharkman since the storm and they're worried about what might have happened to them. They said Reggie and his friends were using his uncle's boat to dive for lobsters. The last anyone had seen of Sharkman, he was out on the water catching fish to bring to the market in Landrail. However, while I was asking questions, I got this strange feeling that something odd was going on with the kids. Someone on Fortune Island had seen them entering a cave just before the hurricane hit, but after the storm passed through, they seemed to have disappeared. Since the cave fills with water during storms, some of the locals think they may have been swept away by the rising waters in the cave and drowned. But I don't think that's what happened."

"I agree. But the question remains: what did happen to them? I think Baka is somehow involved in their disappearances, but how and to what extent remains a mystery."

"Have you any idea how we could find out what happened to them?" Samuel asked.

As Mama Atabei paused to think, she suddenly stopped and smiled. "You know, I just might. There is a wizard with powers much greater than mine called The Seer or Time Traveler. They say he can journey through time and see things the rest of us can't. A friend of mine just recently told me that he's in Haiti. They said his powers are remarkable. Perhaps I can get my friend to tell me where he is and I can pay him a visit."

"Sounds like a person with those powers would be extremely helpful. Maybe I could go with you to help locate this time traveler," Samuel said.

"Thank you for the offer, but I think this is a task I must undertake by myself."

Japapa's Plans

Simone became frozen with fear when she was left alone in the cabin with Japapa. There was no telling what this disgusting, evil man intended to do with her. He was the cruelest human being she had ever met. Closing her eyes, her body began shaking uncontrollably. She stood there and waited for the worst to happen as he slowly moved in her direction.

"W-what do you intend to do with me," she stammered and opened her eyes, the priest's foul-smelling body odor seeping into her nostrils as he drew close enough to touch her.

"That's a good question," Japapa chuckled. "You and the others have caused me a lot of grief. I like the idea of making you my personal slave. At first, I thought I'd turn you over to the crew and have you cook for them, but there is no telling what they might do to you if I did that. Besides, the crew already has someone to prepare their food. On the other hand, as my personal slave, you could be very useful. You can start by swabbng the cabin floor, then wash my clothes, bring me food, wash the dishes, and help bathe and dress me every morning."

"Are you sure that's all you want me to do?" Simone asked sarcastically.

"For now; I'm sure I'll find other valuable services you can render."

Satisfied with his decision, Japapa opened the door and called to one of his crewman. "Get this young lady a bucket of water and a brush," the captain chuckled. "She's agreed to swab my cabin floor. Don't you think that's nice of her?"

"I do indeed," the crewman replied, leering at Simone as he left. A few minutes later, the seaman returned with the water and a brush.

Grumbling to herself, Simone began swabbing the deck while she tried to think of some way to escape. She was hoping that Wendell and Reggie were doing the same.

Chained together below deck, Wendell and Reggie were on the verge of vomiting. The smell of human waste was overwhelming and the groans and pleas for mercy from Black Caesar's Spanish captives were pitiful. Soon, some of these men would be forced to walk off the plank into ocean. Many would eaten by sharks, others would drown, and a few might be lucky enough to be washed ashore on some deserted island. The boys wondered which kind of death would be better: starving in this putrid black hole or being forced overboard with the hope they might be rescued by a passing ship before the sharks ate them.

While they sat in the darkness, sweat pouring from their brows, Reggie asked Wendell again what he knew about the captain, Black Caesar, who was now possessed by their arch enemy Japapa. "Not a lot. In addition to what I told you before, I know he was captured by slave traders who lured him and some of his men aboard their ship. When the ship encountered a hurricane off the Florida coast and was about to sink, one of the black crewmen freed Caesar. Together, they loaded several longboats with guns and ammunition, drifted to the Florida coast, and set up camp. After that, Caesar and some of the other crewmen, used the longboats to attract ships whose captains were not fond of the slave trade. Their intention was to make them believe that they were in desperate need of being rescued. When a ship pulled up alongside, they boarded it and threatened to sink the vessel unless the captain supplied them with all the ammunition, gold and precious jewels they had on board. They employed this ruse for many years amassing quite a large fortune which some people believe is still buried on Elliot Key off the Florida mainland. Caesar evidently killed one of his partners over a woman they had captured and she became part of his harem. Some say Black Caesar had over one hundred women in his harem and all of them were held hostage on his home island. During the early 18th century, he became Blackbeard's lieutenant on the *Queen Ann's Revenge* where the two of them raided American shipping in the mid-Atlantic. After Blackbeard's death, Caesar was taken into custody by the colonial authorities of Virginia, convicted of piracy, and hanged in Williamsburg."

"Wow, despite what you said, you amassed quite a lot of information. I think I'd still rather be dealing wid Black Caesar dan Japapa."

"I agree." Wendell acknowledged. "But we're not. I suspect that Baka is also responsible for transporting us back to this time period. I wonder if we'll ever escape the grasp of this evil devil."

"I'm afraid dat's going ta be quite a challenge. In de meantime, maybe we can learn something useful from de Spanish captive next ta you," Reggie said.

"Maybe, but I'm not very fluent in Spanish."

"You probably know a lot more Spanish dan I do."

"I guess," Wendell admitted. "But right now, I wish I'd paid more attention to my instructor in Spanish class."

"Well, why don't you try talking ta him anyway. De more we can learn, de better chance we have of finding a way ta escape."

"Okay." Wendell agreed and asked their fellow captive how his crew had been captured. After a lengthy response in Spanish, only a portion of which Wendell understood, he learned that Black Caesar and a number of his men had employed the same longboat technique that Wendell had described to Reggie earlier. Their captain, being an honorable man, attempted to rescue the pirates thinking that the seamen in the longboats had been set adrift when their boat sank. Once Black Caesar and his men were on board, they attacked the Spaniards, killing their captain and officers and taking their crew as hostages. Before chaining them up, they invited the crew to remain on the ship and join black Caesar's band of cutthroats. A few accepted the offer; the rest were thrown in the hold and told that they would be dropped off on a deserted island. It was only recently that they realized that some of them would be made to walk the plank.

"*Sabes por que cambiaron de opinion?* (Do you know why he changed his mind?)" Wendell asked.

"*Si. Me entere de que el capitan queria entretener a su tripulacion. Penso que les daria mucho placer ver a algunos de nosotros ahogados o ser comidos por tiburones,*" the Spaniard replied.

"He said that the captain wanted to do this to entertain his crew," Wendell replied. "He thought it would give them a lot of pleasure to watch the captives get eaten by sharks."

"Dat's gross," Reggie said as he shook his head in disgust. "I suspect it wasn't Captain Black Caesar dat changed his mind but Japapa after he took possession of de captain's body. I was hoping de Spaniard would give you some clues dat would help us escape. But it appears dat isn't going to happen. Our only hope is dat Japapa will show us some mercy and maroon us ashore on some deserted island."

"I doubt that will happen," Wendell laughed. "If you remember, he's already said he had plans to sell us as slaves in New Providence."

"Yeah. I forgot about dat. Do you think he's also going ta sell Simone as a slave?"

"Good question. I'm afraid he's too enchanted with her beauty to let her go. My guess is he'll keep her as his own personal slave."

"You're probably right. We've got ta figure out some way ta help her escape before dat happens. Maybe our best chance will be when dey take us ta de slave market in New Providence."

"Maybe," Wendell sighed. "But that's going to be quite a challenge. I was sure we were through with having to deal with that drug-smuggling voodoo priest, but I guess that was a big mistake."

"Yeah, me ta. We'll just have ta focus on one thing at a time and hope dat some opportunity arises dat will enable us ta escape from dis mess we're in."

While the ship slowly made its way to New Providence, the teenagers spent the rest of the day trying to come up with a scheme that would enable them to escape. It wasn't until nightfall of the following day that they felt like they had come up with a solution. Their plan would be risky and it could cost them their lives, but any escape plan was better than working as a slave on a plantation or in a salt mine for the rest of their lives.

Pompeii–Sharkman's Capture

Sharkman woke up to people screaming and the ground floor of the building he was living in shaking beneath his feet. Another earthquake? This would be the fourth one in the last couple of weeks. Getting dressed as fast as he could, he raced outside where he was greeted by a large crack in the road. Leaping over it, he just missed being struck by pieces of brick from the residence next door. Realizing that the harbor was the safest place to be, he ran toward the water's edge where he was quickly joined by others. He could see the fear in people's eyes as they scooted past him in an attempt to get away from the city. Time was growing short. It would only be a couple weeks before Vesuvius's eruption would bring about the destruction of Pompeii.

By the time he reached the boats, things had pretty much settled down, but he knew several, smaller quakes would follow for the next few days. Julius and Antonio motioned to Sharkman and waved him on board their boat. The old man didn't hesitate; he untied one of the mooring lines and leapt onto the vessel. Safely on board, Sharkman was greeted by a smile and slap on the back by the captain. The rest of the boat's mooring lines were then unhitched and the vessel slowly made its way out to sea to begin a day of fishing. When Sharkman looked around at the crew, he could see the relief in everyone's eyes. They all knew it was far better for them to be at sea fishing than spending their time ashore. But they also had to think about their families and hope that they would be safe while they were gone.

Fishing wasn't as good as it had been earlier in the week and Sharkman wondered if the earthquake had something to do with their limited success. When the sun had begun to set and the boat slowly headed back to shore with their modest catch, the old man found a place to sit and begin repairing some of the fishing lines and nets. Hooks needed to be replaced, knots untangled, and frayed lines removed. While he was working, Antonio sat down beside him and pulled out a small piece of parchment. On it, he wrote, "*Quando Capreas abis?* (When will you be leaving for Capri?)" with a narrow quill pen he'd brought on board.

Sharkman took the pen and wrote the word *mox* (soon) and followed it with the question: "*Vis ac familia tua sicut ad me venire?* (Would you and your family like to join me?)"

Nodding his head, Antonio scribbled on the parchment, "I'll ask my father tonight. When do you plan on going?"

When Sharkman let the boy know he hoped to depart on the twenty-first of August, Antonio's face glowed with excitement. Picking up some of the tools lying on the deck next to the old man, the boy began helping Sharkman repair the nets.

When they finished working, Sharkman looked over at Antonio, picked up a piece of parchment, wrote a note, and passed it to the boy. Antonio stared at Sharkman in disbelief. "Y-you can hear and speak?" the boy stammered in Latin.

"Ita (yes), but you must keep it a secret," the fisherman continued in the Latin he learned.

"I will," Antonio promised. "But why have you kept this a secret?"

"I have my reasons. And sometime in the future, I will let you know why I have kept this information from you. For now, only you and I will share this knowledge."

Nodding his head, Antonio stared at the old man and wondered what other secrets he was keeping.

As the sun set, their ship pulled in to shore where they were surprised to find it scraped the bottom as they approached their mooring ring. Julius pondered why the water was so shallow, especially since the tide had been coming in for the last three hours. It should have been easy for them to slowly drift to shore. As Julius puzzled over the issue, Sharkman looked around at the other fishing vessels and noticed that they were all having similar difficulties. Something unusual was happening, something he had never seen before. After helping the crew struggle to get their boat tied up, he decided to spend some time examining the shoreline. At first, he didn't see anything unusual, but when he looked closer, he observed that even though the tide was coming in, the mussels and barnacles growing on the rocks were two feet above the waterline. *How could this be*, he asked himself. *The tide should have covered these life forms by now. According to my estimates and knowledge of the local tidal rotation, it should be a high tide in the morning and these life forms shouldn't be exposed. To confirm this, I will get up early tomorrow and check it out.*

"We can't stay moored here," Julius said to Antonio. "After we unload the fish, I want you and the rest of the crew to help me move the boat into deeper water and anchor it offshore. We can take a yawl with us to bring the men back and forth to the beach."

"What about Sharkman?" Antonio asked his father.

"I'll leave him ashore after we drop off the fish. He can collect the money I negotiated with the owner of the fish house."

Sharkman was waiting to give Julius his money when the crew returned from anchoring the boat offshore. Pleased with the money they received for the day's catch, the captain gave the old man several coins and thanked him for his day's work. Smiling, Sharkman nodded thanks to Julius for his pay and took off to find dinner.

The next morning, Sharkman got up early to investigate the tide and to see if the marine life was still exposed on the pilings. To his dismay, the fishing boats were scraping the bottom of the bay. This meant the land beneath the bay and city was being uplifted. It was a strong indication that the volcano was getting closer to erupting. When he informed Antonio and his father about his observations and concerns about the volcano, they initially laughed at him and told him not to worry. They said they frequently experienced earthquakes, but as far as they knew, only one serious eruption had taken place in the recent past and they were not really concerned that another major one was about to occur. However, when two more large quakes occurred in the city over the next few days, Julius's anxiety increased and Antonio told Sharkman that his family had decided that his suspicions about the volcano erupting soon might be right and they had decided to travel with him to Capri.

It was only two days before Vesuvius was about to erupt and Sharkman was anxious to begin his voyage. Julius and his family had agreed to take the old man on their fishing vessel to Capri and Sharkman was looking forward to joining Antonio and his father on their journey to the island.

As usual, Sharkman arose early, had a breakfast of bread and cheese, and was starting to get dressed when he heard a loud ruckus in the street next to his apartment. Peering out of his window, he spied a number of soldiers shouting to the occupants in the house next door. They were looking for runaway slaves. Someone had told them one was hiding in the vicinity and they had come to capture him.

Since Sharkman had no papers to prove that he was a free man, he knew he was in trouble. Somehow, he had to escape. There was a back door to the building he was living in. If he made it there he could escape through a narrow passageway and hide in the cellar of the building next door. Putting on some clothes, he left his apartment hoping he had enough time to get away. There were no sounds of footsteps behind him when he headed down the passageway. Certain he had not been seen, he entered the cellar and looked for a dark place where he could hide. There were some wooden crates in the corner of the basement, one of which had been recently opened. It was the perfect spot to conceal himself. As he squeezed inside and pressed himself close to the bottom, the shouts of the soldiers searching for slaves grew louder. Trembling with fear, sweat poured down the old man's face, as he waited to see what would happen.

"Someone said they saw him go in this direction," one soldier shouted.

"Check the cellars below the buildings. He could be hiding there."

Pressing his body closer to the bottom of the crate he was hiding in, Sharkman waited. The footsteps of the soldiers were growing louder.

"Look," another soldier shouted, "someone's running down that alleyway."

After the soldiers left, Sharkman remained in the cellar too frightened to move. It was too soon to leave and make his way to the boat, so he took a few minutes to examine the inside of the crate he was hiding in. As his eyes adjusted to the darkness, he became aware that the box he was in was used to store old clothing. That just might provide the advantage he needed. If someone had reported him to the soldiers they would describe him wearing the clothing he had worn the last several days. But if he changed into something that was different, there was chance the soldiers wouldn't recognize him. Quickly getting rid of his old clothes, he slipped into some musty new ones and waited until he could no longer hear any sounds outside the building.

An hour passed before he left the cellar and stepped into the narrow passageway to look around. There were still no signs of any soldiers. The only safe place he could think of hiding was the fishing boat. The question was had they gone out to sea without him. Cautiously making his way down to the harbor, he spotted Julius and Antonio standing by the jolly boat. They hadn't taken off yet and he gave a sigh of relief when they saw him. Racing toward the boat, he waved to them. Halfway to the vessel, two soldiers stepped out from behind a storage shed and grabbed him. *"Non itis usquam servus.* (You're not going anywhere, slave.)"

"Non servus est, (He's not a slave,)" Julius yelled in his defense. *"Piscator est. Navem nostram operatur.* (He's a fisherman. He works aboard our boat.)"

"Videbimus quo, (We'll see about that,)" the soldier replied.

"Ubi sunt chartae tuae? (Where are your papers?)" they asked the old man.

When Sharkman couldn't produce any, they tied his hands behind his back and dragged him away in front of the shocked faces of Julius and Antonio.

"Why have you brought this man to me?" the captain of the Roman guard asked.

"The manager of the apartment reported the old man to us," the soldier replied. "He claimed he's a runaway slave."

"Do you have any proof that you're a Roman citizen?" the captain asked Sharkman.

Pointing to his ears and running a finger across his mouth to indicate he was a deaf-mute, Sharkman sighed and gave the officer a sad look.

"Have you tried to communicate with this man?" the captain asked.

"Yes, but he never said anything. He just kept pointing to his ears and running a finger across his mouth."

"Of course he did, you fool. This man is a deaf-mute. He can neither hear nor speak."

"What do you want us to do with him? He didn't seem to be bothering anybody. From what we were able to learn, he was working as a fisherman on one of the local boats."

Tapping his fingers against the desk, the Roman captain gave the matter some more thought and sighed. "Since he has no papers, put him in a cell for now. I can't imagine anyone wanting to buy a deaf-mute for a slave but you never know."

"Maybe one of our politicians would be interested in purchasing him," the soldier replied. "They're always worried about what secrets people are passing along to others in the government. He would be the perfect person to work for one of them. He seems fit enough and since he can't hear or speak, it's unlikely he'd ever pass along any information."

"Perhaps. I'll see what interest I can generate among them when I go to the Senate meeting this afternoon. In the meantime, have one of the other slaves wash him and place a placard around his neck."

"What do you want us to write on the placard?"

"An interesting question." After mulling it over the captain said, "British slave. Cannot hear or speak."

After he was washed, the soldiers placed a placard around Sharkman's neck indicating he was a deaf-mute and dragged him into the cellar of a military building. The room was packed with other slaves, including women and children, and all of them were naked. When the iron door to the cell was closed, a woman came up to Sharkman and asked what the Romans intended to do with them. Indicating to her that he could neither hear nor speak, she turned to another man and asked the same question.

"*Et intendit vendere us servi,* (They intend to sell us into slavery,)" the man replied.

"*Et filii mei?* (And my children?)"

Erunt forsan servi ut bene, (They will be sold as slaves as well,)" he said sadly.

The conversations Sharkman overheard others having with the woman were heart-rending. Another man told her she would never see her children again. They would be sold to different households and spend the rest of their lives working as slaves for the Romans. If they were lucky, another man said, they would be purchased by one of the rich citizens of Pompeii and treated well. If a lower class citizen bought them, they would have a hard life and probably die at a young age.

While the conversations with the woman continued, Sharkman focused on his own problem. In a short time, Pompeii would not exist, and if he stayed in this city, he would not survive. He hadn't counted on being captured and sold as a slave, so managing to escape the destruction of Pompeii was now an even bigger issue. After several hours passed, he still hadn't come up with a solution to his predicament. Suddenly, several jailors entered his cell and started tying everyone's wrists and ankles with rope and herding them into the marketplace.

The excited citizens of Pompei cheered when the hostages arrived at the city's main square. Shortly after their arrival, the local citizens began inspecting each of the slaves as if they were a piece of meat. A rich nobleman came up to Sharkman and had a jailor open his mouth so he could examine his teeth. Satisfied, the man felt the muscles in Sharkman's arms and legs and then checked the rest of his body to make sure it was not covered with any sores. When he was finished, the nobleman went over to the auctioneer and began discussing how much he intended to ask for the old man. After agreeing on a price, the nobleman moved to the front of the crowd and waited for the bidding to start.

Was this what it was like when Africans were sold in the slave markets in the United States and other countries? It must have been a terrible ordeal, Sharkman thought to himself and shook his head in disgust. *It's a dreadful way to treat human beings.*

Waiting to be placed on the auction block seemed to take an eternity and when the bidding began, intense arguments frequently broke out over who had won the bid and what the final price was. While standing in line, someone came up from behind and grabbed Sharkman's leg. Looking down, he spotted Antonio. The boy gave him a note and disappeared into the crowd. The message told him not to worry. His father was going to try to buy him. The trouble was, would he succeed? He overheard the nobleman agree upon a price with the jailor and it was unlikely Julius would have enough money to outbid him.

"You're next," one of his jailors said to Sharkman and shoved him forward. I know I'm wasting my time telling you this, but I can't resist letting you know how lucky you are. One of the most powerful and wealthy noblemen in Pompeii has already claimed you. He's head of the Senate and it would be unwise for anyone else to try and outbid him."

When Sharkman appeared on the auction block, the crowd grew silent as the Senator stepped forward to make his bid. The amount he offered was extremely high and when the crowd heard the price, they gasped. Sharkman knew that Julius wouldn't be capable of outbidding the Senator, but Julius tried anyway. Shocked by the fisherman's bid, the Senator turned and glared at the man. There was no way he was going to let a commoner outbid him. At that point, he turned to the auctioneer and doubled his bid. The crowd was stunned. Who would pay such a price for a deaf and dumb old man? Even the auctioneer was surprised by what had happened. Stammering, he awarded Sharkman to the Senator before Julius could bid again.

Walking the Plank

"I hope you didn't find the wooden deck of the ship too uncomfortable to sleep on last night," Japapa grinned and looked down at Simone, "As you can see, I have another pile of clothes for you to wash today, but before you do that, I want you to go down to the galley and get me something to eat. I'm starved and I want to feel my best when I meet Blackbeard. I'm planning to get together with him in New Providence. They call it the Republic of Pirates and I understand it's quite a place. I'll enjoy seeing it. Of course, Blackbeard won't recognize me as Japapa. To him, I'll look like his old friend Black Caesar. None of Blackbeard's crew will recognize me either, but I'll remember them. I spent quite a bit of time with them in Baka's fiery cauldron."

Shaking her head in disgust, Simone snapped back. "A pity you had to leave that place. I understand it's really a hot vacation spot. Maybe you'll want to go back to it some time."

"I can see you haven't lost your sense of humor," Japapa snarled. "Unfortunately, for you, I don't plan on returning there anytime soon."

"Too bad," Simone grumbled under her breath as she left the cabin and headed out to get Japapa's breakfast. It was a bright, sunny day with a gentle, easterly breeze and there was quite a commotion taking place on deck as she made her way toward the galley. Curious, she stopped one of Black Caesar's crew and asked, "What's going on?"

"Hasn't the captain told you?"

"No," Simone replied as she stopped to listen.

"Black Caesar has planned some entertainment for us before we reach the Republic of Pirates."

"Did he say what kind?" Simone asked, suspecting that whatever it was it wasn't good.

"He said he was going to take some of our Spanish captives and have them walk the plank. Since this area is infested with tiger sharks, he thought we'd enjoy watching them swim for their lives."

"Is there an island nearby they can swim to?"

"Of course not. It wouldn't be entertaining if there was."

"Has your captain ever done this to his captives before?"

"No. He usually marooned them on some uninhabited island."

"So why do you think he is doing this kind of thing now?"

"He said he's come to realize what brutal people the Spaniards are and as our enemies, they should pay for the lives they've taken. Do you intend to watch?"

"No. The captain said he has other chores for me to do. I'd love to chat with you a little more but I'm already late. The captain has sent me off to get him some food."

Turning to climb down the ladder and pick up Japapa's breakfast, Simone thought about the terrible things the voodoo priest had done to her people in Haiti. Now he was doing the same thing to the Spaniards. *Does this type of cruelty exist in other parts of the world?* she wondered. The more she thought about it the more she realized the answer was "*yes.*" Greed and power often motivated people to do terrible things. After getting a meal of biscuits, beans and fish, Simone returned to the captain's cabin and served the voodoo priest.

"You're late," Japapa snarled. "Next time be more prompt."

"I'm sorry. Do you wish me to leave?"

"No. Sit. We can chat while you watch me eat. It'll be a long time before you'll get any food."

"That's very thoughtful of you." Simone curtsied and sat down.

"You're a snotty little wench. But that's all right; I like my women to be feisty," Japapa laughed.

"Is that what I am? One of your women?"

"For now. Later, I might give you to Blackbeard as a present or sell you as a slave."

"I can't wait."

"Did you hear what I've planned for the Spaniards?

"Yes, one of your crewmen told me about it when I went to get your breakfast."

"They seem quite excited about it, don't you think?"

"I wouldn't say that. Personally, I think what you're doing is disgusting. I don't know why God allows men like you to exist."

"Do you think it matters what God thinks? Baka is my master and protector. In the end, I will succeed because he has blessed me with his presence. It is only his guidance and protection that are important to me."

"Wonderful. When I need help, I think I'll look for it elsewhere. I'm curious, what wretched plans do you have in store for my two friends?"

"You needn't worry about them. They're too valuable to me to feed to the sharks. I can make a lot of money selling two strong, young black boys as slaves. There are quite a few job opportunities for them working in salt mines or planting crops. As my mother once told me, backbreaking work never hurt anyone."

Seeming to have no fear of further retribution, Simone laughed and retorted, "Her advice hasn't seemed to rub off on you. I've never observed you doing a lot of backbreaking work. Can I leave now?"

"Certainly, but before you do, take my plate. I'm finished." Wiping the gravy from around his mouth, Japapa smiled and released a loud belch.

"It'll be a pleasure, Sire." Reaching over Simone took the plate from Japapa and smiled with contempt, "I'm surprised you were able to finish your meal. You're so full of ego, it's hard to believe that there's room in your stomach for anything else."

As Simone turned to leave, Japapa responded with a loud laugh. "Before you go, don't you want to know what I want you to do next?"

"Not really, but I suppose you'll tell me anyway," Simone turned around and glared at the voodoo priest.

"When you go below, collect all the men's plates and scrape everything they didn't eat into a bucket and feed it to the pigs. It's a fitting job for a wench like you, don't you think? You'll find the animals in the bow of the ship. I need to keep them healthy, of course, so I always have something for the men to eat, especially on long voyages. When you finish with the pigs, you'll find several female goats topside. You need to clean their stalls and milk them. My men will need something else for nourishment besides the rum, beer, and wine, they consume when they go to the local tavern."

"What about your clothes? You said you wanted me to wash them before you went ashore."

"That can wait. When you finish with the goats, come back to my cabin. I'll have more things for you to do."

"I can't wait to discover what those 'things' will be," Simone whispered under her breath as she turned and stomped out of the cabin. Somehow, she needed to get in touch with Wendell and Reggie. She wanted to see for herself that they were ok. But she also wanted to find out if they'd come up with an escape plan. So much for their ideas about getting rich. They'd be lucky to get out of this mess alive.

"Wake up." Wendell jabbed Reggie in the ribs.

"What's all de commotion about?" Reggie asked as he watched a couple of pirates drag their Spanish captives on deck.

"From what I understand, today is the day Japapa intends to feed some of his captives to the sharks."

"And does he plan ta include us? De last I heard, he was going ta sell us as slaves."

"That's probably still his plan, but for now I believe he has something else in mind for us."

"Like what?"

"I think he wants us to watch his crew throw their captives overboard and then see the sharks devour them. One of the crewmen told me the captain thought it would be great sport for everyone to see their enemies ripped apart by sharks. He also said he wanted his crew to learn what would happen to them if they disobeyed his orders or stole any of the gold and jewels they pirated from other ships. As far as we're concerned, I think he simply wants to show us what would happen if we tried to escape."

"How thoughtful of him." Reggie shook his head in disgust and took a moment to think. "I doubt we will have any chance ta escape while we're on dis ship. De more I think about it, it seems de best time fer us ta get away will be when dey bring us ta de slave market." Before Reggie could finish formulating his thoughts, the two were unchained, hauled up the ship's ladder, and tossed on to the deck.

"It's so nice to see you again." Japapa laughed and stared at the two terrified young men as they looked up at the priest.

116

"I hope you both had a good night's sleep. I know Simone did."

"Our sleeping arrangements couldn't have been better," Wendell snapped back.

"Well, well, my little sniveler still has some spunk left in him even after the shock of meeting me yesterday. Come along, I want you two to have a front row view of the entertainment."

As one of the crewmen shoved them toward the ship's railing, Japapa motioned to another pirate to force the first of his captive Spaniards to walk the plank. Tears rolled down the cheeks of each of the boys as they watched the man going overboard and cringed as they listened to his screams. It didn't take long for the tiger sharks to rip apart the man's body and the ocean turn blood red. As the carnage continued, both young men tried to look away but Japapa made sure that didn't happen. Forced to watch, Reggie and Wendell clenched their fists and glared at Japapa. The hatred in their eyes only made the priest laugh louder as he ordered another of his crewmen to cast the second Spaniard overboard.

Japapa watched with glee as the last man was made to walk the plank. "Well, it seems we've run out of food and the sharks have lost interest in feeding." Turning around to face his crew, he announced, "The entertainment is over for the day; back to work!"

When the first few captives were cast over the side, there had been loud cheers from the pirates, but their enthusiasm diminished as the slaughter continued. By the time the shark feeding was over, none of the crewmen were making a sound. At that point, Reggie and Wendell saw tears running down the faces of the crew as they returned to their stations below deck, while others seemed to be in shock as they climbed up the ship's rigging.

"Did you enjoy the entertainment?" Japapa asked as he chuckled and ordered one of his crewmen to take the boys below.

"No!" Reggie looked back at the priest with hatred in his eyes. "And I don't think your crew enjoyed it as much as you think."

"Perhaps. But I'm sure they learned a valuable lesson."

Dragged below deck, Reggie and Wendell hung their heads in despair. "Now I can imagine how you felt when you saw your pilot get eaten by sharks after your plane crashed," Reggie sighed and wiped the tears from his face.

"It was just plain awful," Wendell sobbed. "I never thought I'd have to come to grips with what I saw again. I wanted to puke when he ordered those men off of the plank into that school of sharks."

Chained to one another, the two friends had nothing more to say. As they sat in the darkness, there were no thoughts of treasure, only the thought of becoming slaves.

They suddenly heard someone coming toward them and listened carefully. It was hard to make out who it was moving around in the darkness. By the sound of the footsteps, they were certain it was not one of the crew. As the sound came closer, they were relieved to see it was Simone. She was coming down the ship's ladder with an empty bucket.

"Simone," Reggie whispered loudly. "We're over here." Peering into the darkness, she spotted her two friends chained to one another on a wooden bench. Relieved to see Wendell and Reggie, she hurried over and kneeled down next to them.

"I saw the two of you standing by the ship's railing when I was milking goats. I wanted to stay longer to see if anything bad happened to you, but the guard watching over me hurried me along. He wanted me to collect some more scraps of food to feed the pigs. I just finished feeding them for the second time today and was heading back to Japapa's cabin when I decided to stop by and see how the two of you were. Has that beast harmed you in any way?"

"Not physically," Wendell said, "but it was horrible for me to watch those Spaniards being fed to the sharks."

"It was horrible." Reggie agreed. "It was the same kind of thing his minions tried to do to Sharkman. Has he said what he intends to do with you?"

"No. Right now he has me working as his personal slave, but said he might hand me over to Blackbeard as a reward for helping him capture one of the Spanish ships. You never know with him. He might come up with some other evil scheme. Have you figured out a way to escape?"

"We came up with an idea last night, but we're not sure how successful it would be. One thing I know fer certain, we can't attempt ta do anything until we're off of dis ship."

"I might be able to help you," Simone whispered, looking around to make sure no one else was within hearing distance. "The guard that's watching over me has several keys attached to his waist. I believe one of them belongs to the locks connecting your chains together. He doesn't have them clipped too securely to his waist and I might be able to get ahold of them and free you before they take you off the ship."

"Your plan sounds better than anything we've been able to come up with," Wendell admitted. "Let's hope your scheme works. According to the crew, we'll be in New Providence tomorrow morning and Japapa intends to take us to the slave market shortly after we arrive. If he plans to give you to Blackbeard, you just might get an opportunity to steal the keys before the guard realizes it."

"I agree," Reggie said.

"I don't think I'll have any trouble stealing the keys." Simone paused for a second and smiled. "Japapa won't see me do it. He'll be too focused on getting rid of me. By now I'm sure he's sick of all my snide remarks and will be happy to give me to the pirate. I must leave now. I'm already late and Japapa will be looking for me. It's great to see you both," she said before turning and heading up the ladder.

Simone knocked on the captain's door. When no one responded, she knocked again. "Come in," a gruff voice behind the door responded. As Simone entered the cabin, Japapa shook his head in disgust. "Where have you been?"

"I've fed the pigs and goats," Simone responded. "It takes a lot longer than you think. Anyway, I wanted to make sure I got plenty of milk for you. An old goat like you certainly could use it to stay healthy."

"I appreciate your kind thoughts, but as you're well aware, goat's milk is not to my liking. It's primarily for the crew. Now, if you can extract whisky from a goat, I would be eternally grateful."

"The next time I milk them, I'll see what I can do." Simone curtsied and glared back at Japapa while placing the bucket of milk on the deck next to him. "Is there anything else my master would have me do?"

"Of course. As I've noted to some of my other female slaves, a woman must make every effort to appease their master. Some of my clothes need mending. There's a pile of shirts and breeches on the deck next to my desk. You'll find a needle and thread in the cabinet to mend them. You know, if you were more civil to me, life would be a lot easier." Japapa reached out and stroked Simone's hair as she started to turn away.

"I bet." Brushing Japapa's hand away, Simone walked over to the cabinet and picked up some needles and spools of thread.

"Work outside. I need to plan for my meeting with Blackbeard. We are going to discuss my new partnership. I'm sure you won't mind doing that."

Gathering the clothes, she stomped out of the cabin and found herself a place to sit down. She couldn't believe her luck. Simone might not have to steal the keys to help Reggie and Wendell escape. The needles she had just removed from the cabinet might help them do the job. If they didn't, then they could use the pair of pliers she found next to them. However, she'd have to repair Japapa's clothes before she paid the boys another visit.

As Baka reflected on his plans for Sharkman and the teens, he continued to have suspicions that things were not proceeding as intended. *Mama Atabei has once again found a way to meddle in my affairs. How she has done so I'm not quite sure. I thought I knew the limitations of her powers. However, she is a very resourceful woman and has upset my plans more times than I'd like to admit. Perhaps it's time to pay a visit to Japapa and make sure that everything is under control at his end. It will also be good to remind him what will happen if he fails in his mission a second time.*

Sharkman is another matter. I've received word from one of my minions that the old man intends to leave Pompeii before the volcano erupts. This can't happen. To prevent it from taking place, I plan to pay him a visit. If I'm lucky, I might be able to extract the information I need about the temple. None of the priests I've tortured have been willing to give me the temple's location. Perhaps, I can persuade Sharkman to do it before he's enveloped in volcanic ash.

"Has she left?" Baka asked.

"Yes. I sent her outside to mend some clothes."

"I'm impressed by how well Black Caesar's body suits you. Was it comfortable to take possession of him?"

"A lot more comfortable then that pit of boiling tar you tossed me into," Japapa snarled.

Baka gave a hearty laugh and then frowned. "What did you expect? You failed to keep your promise to me. You can't say I didn't warn you."

"No, I have to admit you are a man of your word. What's the reason for this visit?"

"To caution you: I've learned that Mama Atabei intends to rescue the youngsters."

"I don't see how. You already told me she can't travel through time."

"That's true, but I also told you that she is a very clever woman. It appears she's planning to make contact with a powerful wizard called The Seer. He's blind but he has the ability to know what is taking place in our time line as well as in the past and future. In addition, he has the unique skill of being able to transport people through time."

"Wonderful. When can I expect the old crow and this wizard to show up?"

"I'm not sure, but she will be visiting the youngsters and Sharkman very soon. When she shows up here, it is extremely important that you let me know."

"Swell. And how do you expect me to do that?"

Baka reached out and handed Japapa a wooden staff. "Bang this staff three times against the deck and I'll return immediately."

"If you are such a powerful demon and can see everything that's happening in the universe, why would I need anything at all to contact you?"

"Normally, that would be true, but you have to remember that she is a very powerful Haitian priestess and there are times when she can shield her presence from me."

"Too bad I can't do that," Japapa growled.

"Control your tongue!" Baka hissed.

"Do I have a choice?"

"No. I'm just reminding you who's boss."

"I doubt I'll forget that. Whenever Mama Atabei shows up, I'll make sure I summon you."

"Good. I appreciate your thoughtful assistance."

As Baka's image faded, his laughter continued to pound in Japapa ears and his pungent odor lingered in the cabin as the priest thought about the devil and what he would do to him if he failed in this mission. It wouldn't be pretty. Right now, he needed some fresh air and time to think. Trembling, he opened the cabin door and stepped out onto the ship's deck.

When Simone heard Japapa exit his cabin, she looked over at the priest and noticed he was anxious about something. Pretending not to pay attention, she quickly returned to sewing his clothes.

"Have you finished yet?" Japapa asked after stepping alongside her.

"Not yet. There are a lot of repairs to make."

"I suggest you hurry. I have other things for you to do."

"Like what?" Simone inquired.

"You'll find out when you're finished."

"I can't wait."

At that moment, one of crewmen passed by and the captain motioned him to come over. "How long before we reach New Providence?" he asked.

"Half a day at most, especially if the weather holds. We'll certainly be there by tomorrow morning."

"Good. The earlier we get there the better; I need to discuss some things with Blackbeard. I've heard there's a Spanish fleet headed in our direction. If we can band together with his men, we could ambush them. One of my spies has informed me that their ships are laden with gold and silver. If we get to them in time, we'll become even more wealthy."

Surprised that the captain would relay this kind of information to one of his crew, Simone watched the man smile and ask the captain if he could spread the good news among the rest of his men.

"No," Japapa replied. "I'm trusting you to keep it a secret. I'll let the rest of the men know my plans when we are about to attack the ships."

"You can trust me to keep what you told me secret," the crewman replied.

Grinning, the pirate took off, excited about the information that had just been relayed to him.

Turning back to Simone, Japapa smiled. "Good news don't you think?"

"Not if you're a Spaniard aboard one of those ships. Do you think it was wise to tell your crew member of your plan? I can't believe the rumor won't get around New Providence once your men get ashore, especially after they have too much to drink."

"Clever girl."

Eyeing Japapa with suspicion, Simone pondered what had just transpired between the two men. "There is no Spanish fleet laden with gold and silver is there?" she asked.

"Of course not," Japapa laughed. "I just wanted to find out if I could trust the crewman I've just spoken to. If he tells some other crew members, he'll be hanged along with the men he's spoken to. This way, I'll find out which shipmates I can trust when we undertake an important mission."

"A clever scheme, but coming from you, it shouldn't surprise me. Where do you want me to put your clothes when I'm finished?"

"In my cabin," Japapa said and walked away with a smile on his face. After he disappeared from sight, Simone put the clothes in the cabin, gathered some extra needles from the cabinet and headed below deck to give Reggie and Wendell the pliers and needles.

"Shh, don't make any noise," she cautioned as she approached. "Take these needles and the pliers I've brought and see if you can use them to pry open the lock that's keeping you chained together. I think this will be easier than my trying to steal the keys. From what I've heard, you don't have much time. We'll be arriving at New Providence by tomorrow morning. That's when Japapa plans to take you to the slave market. After you get the locks open, leave them in place until you find an opportunity to escape. If you're successful, I'll hear about it from Japapa. He doesn't like being fooled. He'll send his most trusted men after you. When he does, I'll try to make my escape. I haven't figured out yet where we can meet up, but when I find a safe place to hide, I'll try to get a message to you. I must leave now. I'm running out of time. Japapa is very suspicious about everything I do. Good luck!" Smiling, she turned around, kissed each of them on the cheek and climbed the ladder leading to the main deck.

Simone was gone before Reggie and Wendell could thank her. Taking the metal tool and needles she had given them, they immediately began working on the locks, hoping they could get them open before daybreak.

Mama Atabei Visiting The Seer

"Have you found where The Seer lives?" Mama Atabei asked James, her most trusted follower.

"Yes. He is hiding in the mountains. He's afraid the country's current leader intends to torture him for information."

"What kind of information are they looking for?"

"I don't know exactly, but one of his close followers claims he knows the location of a large deposit of gold that the French left behind when they fled the country."

"If that's the case, I'll need to get in touch with him as soon as possible. How soon can you take me to his hideout?"

"I can take you there in a couple of days. However, we must leave at night to avoid his enemies spotting us."

"I understand. It's too bad we can't leave sooner."

"I agree. But in two days, there will be a festival in the city and most people will be celebrating the island's victory over the French. I suspect that the men who have been sent to find him will be more interested in participating in the festivities than hunting The Seer down."

"Then two days from now is when we'll go."

Prior to their day of departure, heavy rains had soaked the mountain passes and Mama Atabei had a difficult time following James along the slippery, muddy trails that led to The Seer's hiding place. Both were out of breath when they reached The Seer's house, and when James knocked on the door, there was no response. Knocking a second time, they heard a weak, trembling voice invite them in. After entering, they found a wrinkled old man seated in a dark corner of the room. Looking around, Mama Atabei noticed that there was very little furniture in the house and the building had a strange odor. She'd smelled that odor in the past. It was the unmistakable smell of death.

"*Bon aswè, non mwen se Mama Atabei.* (Good evening, my name is Mama Atabei.)"

Standing, The Seer said, "It is not necessary to speak to me in Haitian-Creole. I understand and speak English very well."

"Good. That will make it easier to talk with you about my problem."

"Please sit down," The Seer said in a low, raspy voice. "There are a couple of chairs in the corner. Bring them closer so we can hear one another better. I can't hear very well and I've been nearly blind since I was a youngster so it helps me to be close to the people I'm speaking to."

After placing the chairs in front of The Seer, Mama Atabie and James sat down and stretched their weary bones. The old woman was grateful to have a chance to rest and catch her breath after hiking the muddy trails that led up through the mountains. The man she was sitting in front of was so thin he looked like a living skeleton. He had no hair on the top of his head, his eyes were shrunken in his head and clouded over, and a scraggly cluster of hair clung to the tip of his chin.

"I am here to ask for your help. My friends, three teens and an old fisherman from Crooked Island, are missing. It's been a while since anyone has heard from them and I suspect that Baka has had something to do with their disappearance."

The Seer nodded. "You are right to be concerned about your friends. They are in serious trouble and it will be difficult for you to rescue them, especially if Baka is involved."

"Can you tell me where they are? And if there's a way I can save them?"

"You are a powerful priestess, but this time you will not be able to rescue them so easily. I regret to say they no longer share this time period with us."

"Not in this 'time period'? What do you mean by that?"

"Baka has sent them into the past. Sharkman is in Pompei just days away from being smothered in volcanic dust. The youths have been captured by the pirate, Black Caesar, who is now possessed by your old friend Japapa. He intends to give Simone to Blackbeard where she will become part of his harem; he's decided to sell the boys off as slaves. After he does, they will either work in the salt mines in Bonaire or plow fields and raise crops for the British Loyalists who have fled to the

Bahamas. If this happens, I'm sure neither one of them will survive very long."

"How can you know all this?"

"I may be almost blind, but in a way my blindness has become my most valuable gift. It has enabled me to see things other people cannot."

"Now I know what you mean when you say it will be difficult for me to rescue my friends. My powers are great but, unlike yours, I can't see things that are happening in the past nor can I travel through time."

"Fortunately, there are ways for you to do both and I will be happy to show you how. I believe we can work together to save your friends."

"You said 'we'. Does that mean that you are willing to journey with me and travel back through time to save my friends?"

"Yes. Even though I'm old and can hardly see, when I travel back through time my strength and ability to see improve greatly. In many ways, I become a young man again and my powers improve immensely."

Mama Atabei was shocked by what The Seer had just said. Taking hold of the old man's hand, the priestess helped The Seer stand and said, "If what you say is true, I think we should begin our journey back in time immediately."

"Before we take a look into the past, I'm curious about something," The Seer inquired as he continued to hold Mama Atabei's hand.

"And what is that?" the priestess asked.

"Why are you are so interested in saving the youngsters and Sharkman? They're not related to you; I believe you have other reasons for wanting to save them. I would like to know what those reasons are before we undertake our journey back in time."

Could she trust the powerful wizard? Mama Atabei didn't know. She had so many enemies, it was difficult to determine which of her so-called friends would slit her throat and which would reach into boiling water to save her life. If her plan to save her friends was going to work, she had no choice but to trust The Seer.

"You're right. I do have a plan. As you are aware, Haiti is once again in turmoil. People are rioting in the streets. There is not enough food for them to eat. The last earthquake that struck the island has left a lot of the residents homeless, and then there was the recent hurricane. The country needs new leadership. I believe that their new leader should be Simone's father, Claude Joseph, but I doubt he will leave his job in the Bahamas without his daughter."

"I know of Claude Joseph. You're right. He would be the man to become the new president of Haiti. But it will take our combined powers to make this happen. In order to begin our journey, I want you to take my hand and concentrate. We are going to begin by looking into the past and trying to see through the darkness that surrounds us. We are going to start our journey by going back to Pompeii, to the time just before Mt. Vesuvius's famous eruption, to see if we can locate Sharkman. We won't be able to rescue him at this point, but we can see what is happening to him and begin to make plans that will prevent him from being burned alive in volcanic ash.

"Where are we?" Mama Atabeii asked The Seer as she tried to adjust to her surroundings.

"At a place where time and distance have merged into one."

"I can feel your presence, but I can't see you."

"That's because no light can penetrate this part of the universe. We have entered a black hole between two parallel universes. At this moment, they are slipping past one another. From here, we can see both the past and the future. To the left, the earth is moving into the past and to the right it's racing toward the future, and it is a place where Baka cannot see us. He can sense our presence and he knows we are meddling in his affairs, but he does not know exactly where we are and what we're up to."

"I'm glad to hear that," Mama Atabei said with a sigh of relief. "Baka is a dangerous adversary."

"Now, I want you to concentrate. Look deep into the darkness. Do you see Sharkman?"

"I can feel his presence but I can't see him."

"Then you must concentrate more. Bring his face into focus, then try to envision the rest of his body."

Slowly, Sharkman appeared in front of her. He was chained to a wall in a dark cellar.

"Where is he?" Mama Atabei asked.

"He appears to be in the cellar of a wealthy Roman household. Someone has purchased him as a slave. I can't quite make out who that person is but I know that your friend's life is in danger if he remains where he is. Soon, the entire city of Pompeii will be destroyed when Mt. Vesuvius erupts. The place where your friend is being kept captive will soon be buried in pumice and volcanic ash."

"Is there anything we can do to save him?"

"Possibly, but it has to be done in a way that will not change the timeline he is currently journeying through. If it does, his future may be altered."

"I understand. But I need your help to accomplish this. Please! Quickly! Sharkman's survival is important to me."

"I understand," The Seer responded.

As The Seer reached into the fabric of time, Mama Atabei felt something ripple through her body. She held on tightly to The Seer and prayed that the wizard would save her friend.

Pompeii–Baka and Sharkman

Sharkman sat quietly on the cellar floor. The chains that secured him to the wall were cutting into his wrists and for the moment, he saw no way to escape. The damp, musty room was a haven for rats who were constantly running up to sniff him. They would soon decide he was something good to eat and start gnawing at his flesh. A shiver of fear ran through his body as he thought about what it would be like to be eaten alive. He also began to think about the times when he was a soldier in Vietnam and the horrible things that had happened to his platoon members when he was there. He would never forget those experiences. Most of all, he remembered the rats. At night, driven by hunger, these creatures would often scurry out of the jungle and chew on the soldiers who had been wounded in action during the day. Ironically, today, roasted rats were a prime source of protein for some people who lived in Asian countries.

Alerted by footsteps coming into the cellar, Sharkman looked up and saw a middle-aged gentleman wearing a toga. "I hope you're not too uncomfortable," the man said as he looked down at him and smiled. "I also hope you appreciate the clothes I've provided to keep you warm. For a brief moment, I thought your friend would outbid me in the slave market. Thankfully he didn't. It was fortunate that the guards made me aware that they had captured a deaf-mute. They thought you would be the perfect person to become one of my household servants since you wouldn't be able to pass along information about things that were happening in my home or in the Senate. Once they told me about you, I knew immediately who they were talking about. We both know that you're not a deaf-mute; you can hear and speak quite well. And there is no need for you to speak to me in Latin since we both know you're very fluent in English."

A look of disgust briefly passed across Sharkman's face before he sighed and said, "I should have guessed you were the one who was bidding for me. I think I preferred you in the last body you possessed. You were much more appealing as a pig."

"I don't know about that," Baka laughed. "I think becoming an elegant member of the Roman Senate is much more suited to someone of my status."

"If you say so. Now, what exactly do you want and what do you intend to do with me?"

"Want? I would like you to tell me the location of the temple you discovered in Vietnam. If you do, it will make things so much easier for both of us. I suspect it's not in your nature to do that. Consequently, I'll just keep you chained to the wall of this cellar. As you are already aware, there are a lot of hungry rats in this basement and I'm sure they would enjoy gnawing on your body."

"You're right! I'll never tell you where that temple is. Telling you its location would betray the trust of the men I trained and fought with. They believed, as I do, that the temple is a sacred place whose primary purpose is to provide its priests with a place where they can focus on eradicating evil from this world. I'm sure everyone on this planet would be happy to see that happen. I, for one, would be especially pleased, since there's no one more evil than you that I would like to see eliminated."

"I always suspected that you were too much of an idealist to tell me the temple's location so I'm just going to leave you with the rats and the terrible destruction the volcano is about to inflict on this city. This cellar will soon become filled with hot ash and pumice. Delightfully, when that happens, you will burn and suffocate."

"I shouldn't have expected anything less from you." Once again ignoring Baka's request for information, Sharkman asked, "So, where are my teenage friends?"

"There's no need to worry about them. I've resurrected Japapa and he's been overjoyed at being able to get his revenge on that trio."

"It appears you've thought of everything."

"Not quite everything. I still have Mama Atabei to deal with. She is beginning to meddle in my affairs again and I need to find some way to eliminate her. I assume your silence also means that she has not been in contact with you and that you have no idea what her plans are. I'll leave you to your demise. Have fun. I'm sure we'll meet again in the afterlife."

"Not in any afterlife you're part of," Sharkman grumbled and watched Baka disappear up the steps leading from the basement.

"What's happening?" Mama Atabei asked.

"Watch carefully." Reaching into the past, The Seer stirred the fabric of time. Flashes of colored light spread in every direction as the ground beneath Mama Atabei's and The Seer's feet continued to tremble. "Pompeii is about to be destroyed," The Seer announced.

Awakened by movement beneath his feet, Sharkman realized the city was experiencing another earthquake. The cellar was beginning to crumble around him and cracks in the floor began to spread open under his feet. He yanked against his chains and to his surprise, they shook free from the cellar wall. But he still needed to remove the chains and iron shackles attached to his wrists and feet. Looking around the cellar, he spotted a hammer. It was just what he needed. The room continued swaying under his feet as he stumbled toward the hammer, picked it up, and began slamming it against the point where the chain was secured to his wrists. Nothing happened. He oriented the chains in a different position and slammed harder. Still nothing. The chain finally cracked open on his third try. He then used the hammer to free the shackles from his legs just as pieces of the ceiling began to topple into the cellar. There wasn't much time left. He needed to escape now or he would be buried under a pile of debris. Remembering the stairs leading up from the cellar, he hurried toward them just as another violent tremor shook the building and threw him to the ground. As he scrambled to get up, he reached out for the steps. They were still intact. As fast as he could, he made his way to the main floor of the building where he heard people screaming and saw them running in different directions. The intensity of the earthquake had panicked the entire population. People were abandoning their homes and fleeing into the streets. Some were running toward the waterfront with their children; others were headed into the Colosseum. Blending in with the crowd, he raced toward the harbor. Sharkman hoped to be able to meet up with Julius and Antonio once he got there.

He was relieved when he spotted the captain and his son waving to him. Waving back, he ran toward Antonio and pulled him aside. "We need to leave now! Vesuvius is about to erupt and Pompeii is doomed! Are you ready to go?" Sharkman shouted in Latin.

"No, my father wants to take the crew and their families along with us."

"Then he needs to hurry up and get them!" Sharkman urged.

"Take one of the jolly boats out to our fishing vessel and hide there while we're gone," Antonio suggested.

Sharkman watched with apprehension as the captain and Antonio left to round up the rest of his crew and their families. *Will we be able to escape before the eruption begins?* he wondered. He wasn't so sure they would.

"Will they make it?" Mama Atabei asked The Seer as she watched Sharkman's attempted escape play out.

"We must wait and see. They seem to be a resourceful lot. In the meantime, assuming they do, I must figure out a way for us to travel back in time, to rescue Sharkman, and bring him back to the present. As you might imagine, that will not be easy to accomplish.

Pirate Ship–Planning for Escape

"Once again you're late; I assume you've finished your tasks," Japapa snarled as he paced back and forth in his cabin.

Simone smiled and curtsied. "Yes, Master, I've finished everything you asked me to do."

"Good, your master will introduce you to Blackbeard tomorrow. He has an eye for beautiful young girls. Tonight you can sleep out on the deck again, but I want you to clean up in the morning. While you're out there, I'd keep an eye out for some of my crew members. They haven't seen a beautiful young lady like you in a long time and there's no telling what they might do."

"How thoughtful of you to let me sleep outside with them. Maybe I'll be able to convince one of them to dispose of you," Simone snapped at Japapa.

Laughing at her retort, Japapa ordered Simone to leave. "I doubt you'll be able to lure one of those weaklings to do that. Go. I need to get some sleep." Yawning and stretching his arms, he remarked, "It really is going to be a beautiful evening outside. I hope you enjoy looking at the stars on a night like this."

Slamming the cabin door behind her, Simone stepped into the cool night air and looked for a place to sleep. While searching for an appropriate location, she spied a young man leaning over the railing of the ship staring into the water. Curious, she stepped alongside him, introduced herself, and asked , "What are you looking at?'

"Those balls of light that appear in the ship's wake. Have you ever seen them before?"

"I saw them once when I went fishing with my father. It was late at night and we were headed out to the coral reef near our village to catch snapper. My father told me that the balls of light were created by marine creatures called a ctenophores. He said they were harmless and only generated light when the boat's wake agitates them."

"You're lucky to have had a father who knew so much. Mine was killed by a band of ruthless thugs. They also killed my mother, ransacked our house, stole most of our precious possessions, and left me for dead. Black Caesar found me a few days later, and when he saw what had happened to my family, he made me a member of his crew. I always liked Black

Caesar. He was never cruel to me and I never remember him being ruthless, like he was today. Whenever he captured sailors from other ships, he'd either offer them a chance to become a member of his crew or put them ashore. Today was horrible. I never saw him make men walk the plank so they would be eaten by sharks. Over the last few days, he seems to have become a different person. It was terrible to stand there and listen to the horrible screams of those men as they were being devoured by these creatures. Do you think Black Caesar is evil and could do things like that to us in the future if we didn't obey his orders?" the young man wanted to know and lifted his head to look at Simone. When he did, she noticed a deep scar etched across his cheek and wondered how he'd gotten it.

"I do," Simone replied. "A person who does something like that can't be trusted. You can never tell when they'll turn on you. Did Black Caesar put that scar on your face?" Simone added as an afterthought.

"No. The Black Caesar I knew wouldn't do something like this. It was one of the pirates that raided the homesite where I lived. I think you're probably right. Our captain has become an evil person," the young sailor said and shook his head. "When I arrive at New Providence, I've decided to jump ship. I've talked to some of the other crew members and they've decided to do the same. They have heard about a safe house at the south end of the island where we can hide until Black Caesar's ship leaves port. We plan to stay there until we can board another ship and get dropped off in America. I understand it's a country where we can get a new start in life."

"I heard that too!" Excited by the thought she had found a way for Reggie, Wendell and her to escape, Simone decided to see if the young man would be willing to take them along. "Black Caesar intends to sell me and my friends as slaves. Ever since we've been captured, we've been trying to think of a way to escape. Is there any chance my friends and I might join you and the other crew members when you make your escape?"

"I don't know if the others will let you in on our escape plans. But I'll talk to them and see if they would be willing to take you with us. By the way, my name's Roger," the young man offered with a smile.

"Thanks, mine is Simone. If your friends agree, I'll pass the word along to my friends. This really gives me some hope."

While pretending to be asleep, Simone waited for the ship's guards to nod off so she could sneak below deck to talk to Reggie and Wendell. That moment seemed like it would never come. Finally, two of the guards left their posts to investigate a loud noise coming from the bow of the ship. It was now or never. Jumping up, she climbed down the ship's ladder into the hold and anxiously looked for Reggie and Wendell while trying not to wake up any of the other ship's prisoners. After searching the sleeping quarters, she found them chained together in one of the lower bunks. "Wake up," Simone whispered in Reggie's ear and shook his shoulder. When he didn't respond, she shook him harder. "Wake up," she whispered louder. "I've got something important to tell you."

Reggie yawned, wiped the sleepers out of his eyes and asked, "Simone, what are you doing here?"

"I think I've found a better way for us to escape."

More alert when he heard about the good news, Reggie asked, "How?"

"Several of the crewmen didn't like it when the captain fed the prisoners to the sharks. They said he never did anything like that before and they were afraid that he could do similar things to them in the future if they didn't obey his orders. When the ship lands in New Providence, they intend to jump ship. One of them told me they are going to a safe house on the other side of the island where they will hide and hopefully hook up with another captain who will take them to the Americas."

"Do you believe his story?" Reggie asked suspiciously.

"I do. Right now he's talking to the others involved in this plot to see if they'll agree to take us along with them. Have you been able to unlock yourselves from the chains with the tool I provided?"

"Yes. I just hope de crewmen agree ta take us with dem. I don't think our chances fer escape are very good if we try ta do it on our own. And I'm sick of de bilge rats. They nibble on de food dey give us ta eat and sometimes crawl across us at night. I don't know when dey will start feeding on Wendell and me."

"Bilge rats! You didn't tell me about them!" Simone shivered.

"We've got ta get off dis ship. Der's no telling if Japapa will change his mind and decide to feed us ta de sharks."

"I agree," Simone said. "If these crewmen let us go with them, I'll find out how they intend to sneak us off the ship. Once I know, I'll pass the information along to you. I'm sorry. I can't stay any longer. Japapa and his crew are always watching me. Right now, they expect me to be sleeping outside his cabin.

If his crew on watch comes back and I'm not there, they'll report it to Japapa and that will be the last I'll see of you."

Quietly making her way back to the deck near Japapa's cabin, Simone looked around to make sure no one was watching, then lay down and pulled a wool blanket over her body. Above her, the Milky Way stretched across the evening sky creating a brilliant stream of comforting light, while the gentle rocking of the ship slowly lulled her to sleep.

Watching Simone close her eyes, Japapa chuckled and shook his head. Did Simone really think she could put something over on him? Once, maybe, but not a second time. There was no way she and her friends were going to escape. He couldn't wait to see the expressions on their faces when he snared them in his cleverly devised trap.

Escaping Pompeii

Sharkman couldn't sleep. It was 2:00 p.m. and he could hear Mount Vesuvius rumbling in the distance. Getting up, he left his hiding place and came up on the deck to watch Julius's crew and their families begin to board the fishing boat. The ground near the shore was beginning to crumble and the old man was glad to see the last person make it on board. Pulling up the ship's anchor, the crew hoisted the vessel's sail and quickly started to row out to sea. Looking back, they could see broad sheets of fire and ash spewing from the mouth of the volcano and the buildings in the city collapsing into cracks generated by earthquakes. Fires had begun in several places and a snowflake-like layer of ash and pumice had begun to blanket the city.

People continued running out of their houses into the streets screaming. The crew and their families could see hundreds of people standing at the waterfront screaming for them to come back. Children were desperately waving their arms hoping someone would see them. Some were jumping in the water to escape the hot ash.

Julius knew he couldn't go back. He had too many people aboard his vessel already. In addition, the seas had started to get rough and the wind was blowing in the wrong direction. It was all the crew could do to guide the boat away from the city.

The volcano erupted again late in the afternoon. This time, the eruption was so violent that a tremendous shock wave slammed into the boat and threw the captain and his passengers onto the deck. Another plume of ash and pumice was jettisoned into the sky and boulders of molten rocks were flung into the sea. Pleading with his men to row harder, Julius's vessel was unable to escape some of the heated rocks that were being hurled toward them. Fires began to break out in several places on the deck and he ordered his men to stop rowing and start throwing buckets of sea water on the flames.

"I don't know if we can survive this," Julius cried out to Antonio. "I've never seen anything like it."

"I know," Antonio replied as he dumped another bucket of seawater onto the burning frame of the boat. "We're lucky to be this far out at sea. Most of those molten boulders can't reach us out here."

"One more is way too many," Julius responded. "If we get hit by a few more, there won't be enough of us to put out the fires and our vessel will sink."

Fortunately, the tide eventually turned in their favor and took them farther away from Pompeii and the burning boulders being flung into the air. When the fires on the ship were under control, the crew and Sharkman took a few moments to look back at the city. It was now completely ablaze and rivers of lava were streaking down the sides of the volcano. Staring back at the inferno, the crew gasped in shock as a huge cloud of ash hanging over the volcano collapsed from its own weight and completely smothered the city in six super-heated waves of hot ash. At that point, nearly all of the people remaining on the shore were incinerated.

Julius and his crew watched in silence. Tears flooded many faces. Friends and families they had known all their lives had vanished. There was little doubt their Roman gods were angry with them; otherwise, why would they ever let this terrible thing happen. And why were they still alive? Why didn't they die as well? They would be eternally grateful for the old fisherman who had saved their lives. But it would be hard to forget the destruction of their homes and the loss of their friends.

Sharkman knew there was no answer to their questions. When soldiers he fought with died in battle, he also wondered why he had lived and they didn't. Was there some special reason God had let him survive? He guessed he would never know the answer. Grief was always hard to get over, and when he watched Pompeii disappear in a cloud of hot ash, the pain generated by the war and the loss of his family came back to haunt him with memories he was still trying hard to forget.

Watching the tragic disappearance of his city, Julius ordered his crew to start guiding their vessel toward the island of

Capri. Hopefully, the island's residents would welcome them and would let them begin rebuilding their lives.

Mama Atabei and The Seer

"I thought I'd seen terrible things during my life, but what just happened to Pompeii and its residents was horrific, "Mama Atabei confessed.

"I agree, but people have suffered through worse," The Seer acknowledged.

"I know," Mama Atabei admitted, "but it's still horrible."

"The man you are trying to rescue seems to be a very honorable person. I'm curious about something: why are you trying to save him before the youngsters?"

"I've told you before; his survival is critical to my plans."

"Yes, but that doesn't answer my question."

"Is it necessary for you to know everything?" the old woman inquired.

"If I am going to be able to bring Sharkman back to the future, I must know everything about him. I don't want anything he's done to disrupt the timeline and make it difficult for me to rescue him and the teens."

Mama Atabei remained silent for several minutes before answering.

"He served as a soldier in the Vietnam War. His real name is Jeff Mason. He was very young when he enlisted and extremely brave. He even signed up to go back to the war zone more than once. During his last tour of duty, he discovered an ancient temple in the jungle while he and his men were on patrol. Most of the temple was covered with vines and other growth making it difficult for them to determine what the structure was, but after looking around its perimeter, one of Jeff's men found a door that led to a passageway that let the troops enter the structure. It became apparent that even though the temple was hidden in the jungle, someone was still using it. Initially, they thought it was enemy troops, but that turned out not to be the case. Jeff and his men were stunned by what they saw inside. There were beautiful paintings and statues in each of the rooms they searched. The artwork told stories about how each of the world's religions began; the literature they uncovered in different languages revealed that the priests' primary mission was to eradicate the evil spreading throughout the world. Ultimately, Jeff and his men realized the temple was still a gathering place for religious leaders and decided it should be protected. He told his commanding officer about what they discovered when he returned to headquarters and told him why the temple should be protected. Initially his commanding officer wanted to use the building for a command post, but Jeff talked him out of it and he agreed with Jeff to keep the temple's purpose and location a secret until the war was over and its religious leaders could return.

"Unfortunately, one of the locals found out about the temple. This man quickly informed the village chief who told Jeff's commander he wanted to visit the site. Jeff argued with the head of the village that it would be best if the temple's location was kept a secret, but the village chief disagreed and insisted on seeing it. Frustrated, Jeff finally agreed to take him to the temple. The next day, Jeff's small platoon and the chief met and headed toward the temple. On the way there, they were ambushed. Everyone, including Jeff's commanding officer and the village chief, was killed and Jeff was taken prisoner. He was tortured for weeks by the North Vietnamese. They wanted information about his military operation as well as the location of the temple, but Jeff refused to tell them anything. When they finally accepted that he would never reveal anything useful, they sent him to prison in North Vietnam.

"While he was there, his wife and two children were burned to death. Someone had purposely set fire to their house when the family was sleeping. The police never found out who did it, and Jeff didn't learn about their deaths until he was released from prison and his new commanding officer informed him. When he returned home, his parents took him to his family's grave site. It was a heartbreaking experience Jeff would never forget. He remained in the town where he was raised for a while and worked in his father's business, but eventually he decided to leave. Jeff couldn't bear staying in the hometown where his family had died. For the next couple of years, he moved from one town to another doing odd jobs. Then one day, he met some of his old army buddies who told him they were headed to the Bahamas to become shark fishermen. They said he could make a lot of money and asked if he would like to join them. After giving it some thought, he decided to go. I suppose in some ways becoming a shark hunter was his way of escaping what had happened to his family and the memories he carried with him about the war.

"He spent several years hunting sharks and made good money at it but eventually decided to give up shark fishing. He told his friends he had experienced enough cruelty in his life and killing sharks only added to some of the terrible things he'd seen during the war. He said that during his time as a shark fisherman he'd begun to see the important role these creatures played in their environment and decided he should do something to protect them. Eventually, he succeeded and stopped their senseless slaughter. After that, he became a commercial fisherman on Fortune Island. It was there that he met up with the youngsters."

"That's quite a story," The Seer admitted with a frown. "But there's still more to the tale isn't there?"

Mama Atabei gave another long pause before nodding.

"And it has something to do with Baka and the temple Jeff and his platoon discovered in the jungle in Vietnam?"

"Yes."

"What is it about the temple that concerns Baka so much?"

Mama continued, "He sees it as a threat to his control over the evil forces in this world. He feels that if he doesn't destroy the temple soon, the priests will return and continue their mission of trying to wipe out evil. Baka's problem is that the priests keep cloaking its location."

"I see, hence the urgency to save Sharkman as soon as you can. In a way, you might say the fate of the world is in his hands."

Mama Atabei agreed. "And Baka will not make our efforts to save the old man easy. Fortunately, the priests generated a protective shield that's still in place. That is why I need to rescue the old fisherman. Baka will do anything to get the temple's location from him: torture him in the most horrible ways you can imagine or threaten to kill his friends. He's already done some of those things and failed. I don't know how much more Sharkman can take."

"So why doesn't Baka get the temple's location from one of the villagers the soldiers encountered? Surely one of them has discovered its location by now."

"Because all of the villagers were killed in a bombing raid during the last days of the war."

"Now I understand why it's so important to save Sharkman. It might take a little while, but don't lose faith. I'm sure within a few days I'll be able to rescue him."

Escaping the Pirate Ship

"Wake up." Roger gently shook Simone's shoulder. Rolling over, she rubbed her bleary eyes and looked at the young man.

"We've just lowered anchor in New Providence and my friends and I have decided we need to make our escape now. You and your companions are welcome to join us, but we can't wait for you. I've written the location of the safe house where you and your friends can meet up with us. I've also given you the directions on how to get there. Commit the information to memory and have your friends do the same. When you have finished, destroy the paper. It won't be good for you or us if anyone finds this information in your possession."

"I understand," Simone agreed and picked up her blanket.

"I had hoped you and your friends could join us but we have to go now. If you expect to escape, you must get off the ship quickly. There's not a lot of time left."

Before Simone realized it, Roger disappeared into the shadows. After reading the information on the piece of paper, she committed it to memory, and scurried below deck to inform Reggie and Wendell of the plan.

"We thought you'd never get here," Wendell replied anxiously. "We heard them drop the anchor a short while ago and wondered if you were still coming."

Simone handed Reggie and Wendell the instructions she'd received from Roger and told them that they had to memorize the information and then destroy the paper. "Do it as quickly as you can. You must leave now before the morning light increases. Unfortunately, I can't go with you. The three of us can get together later. If for some reason I can't escape from Blackbeard, don't wait for me. Head inland toward the safe house. I'll find some way to escape and hook up with you."

"Why can't you come with us?" Wendell asked as he unlocked the iron shackles around Reggie's wrists.

"If I come with you now, Japapa will become suspicious and check on you. I've got to make sure he doesn't do that. His plans for you remain the same. He still wants to sell you as slaves. I'm not sure what he'll decide to do with me yet—give me to Blackbeard or keep me for himself. I doubt he'll do the latter. When he gives me some more tasks to do, I'll try to slip away and meet up with you at the safe house."

"I don't like your plan," Wendell grumbled. "If it fails, you could be in a lot of trouble. Suppose you can't get away and Japapa turns you over to Blackbeard?"

"You worry too much," Simone said and gave her friends an insincere laugh. "Now go, or both of you will wind up becoming slaves."

"We'll get going," Reggie retorted, "but I'm not happy about your plan either."

Reggie and Wendell climbed up the ladder, quietly slipped over the side of the ship, and made their way to the beach.

"Should we wait for her?" Wendell asked.

"No," Reggie responded. "You heard what she told us ta do. If we stay, we risk getting caught. Our best hope is fer her ta escape and meet up wid us later at de safe house."

"And what are the odds that she'll be able to join up with us?" Wendell asked.

"Not good," Reggie admitted and shook his head. "I wish you would stop harping on things dat may or may not happen. If we are successful in getting away, den we will have a chance ta help her."

Simone and the young men's plans were pretty risky Mama Atabei acknowledged. As she watched the trap that was being prepared for her friends by Japapa unfold, she realized she could do nothing at the moment to help them. If the youngsters didn't figure out what the evil priest was up to real soon, they would all be in deep trouble.

Meanwhile, she and The Seer were keeping watch over Blackbeard and discovered he had plans of his own regarding Black Caesar.

Over the years, Blackbeard remained aware of the exploits of Black Caesar and he had decided it would be to his advantage to make him a member of his crew. He couldn't elevate him to the position of master boson; Black Caesar would take that kind of a move as an insult. The best way to handle the situation was to elevate the man to the position of First Lieutenant. If he did, there was no doubt Black Caesar would be pleased with the move and he would become wealthy aboard the *Queen Anne's Revenge.* As Blackbeard pondered this idea further, he ordered another draft of rum from the barmaid and found himself a comfortable chair to sit down on in the corner of the tavern. While he was staring at a woman across the room, one of his crewmen approached and asked permission to speak. "I've got some news," he said excitedly.

"And what news would that be?" Blackbeard snarled. "Can't you see I'm trying to think about something very important."

"I'm sorry, sir, but I thought you'd be overjoyed with the information I've got to tell you."

"It better be something really good, otherwise I'll have the skin flayed off your back in front of the crew."

"It is, Captain, I swear."

"Then out with it. I don't have time to listen to you babble all day."

"Black Caesar is giving you a gift of a beautiful black woman. Everyone says she would make a fine addition to your harem. They've told me her beauty is more breathtaking than any of the other young ladies you have."

"That is good news." Blackbeard smiled with delight. Getting up from his chair, he gave the man a pat on the back and ordered the barmaid to give his crewman a jug of rum. Now he had even more reason to make Black Caesar a member of his crew. Leaving the tavern, he headed toward the harbor to greet his future lieutenant.

Capri Arrival

Antonio watched the flying fish glide just above the water's surface as his father's vessel continued to head southwest toward the island of Capri. He hoped the residents of this island would allow his father to fish along its waters and wondered where they would find a new place to live. His father and Sharkman could live on the boat with him for a while, but the vessel was too small to provide living quarters for the rest of their crew and their families. If the local residents didn't have homes large enough to share with the crew, maybe there would be a large land holder on the island who would sell the families property where they could build their own houses. Antonio already knew his father hoped to build a home and a fish house on the island where he could process and sell their fish.

Earlier in the day, Julius had told the crew they were headed to the city of Marina Grande on the island of Capri. He said he didn't know a lot about the place but after he talked about it with other fishermen in Pompeii, they told him it was a good fishing location and that the fishermen that lived there made a good living from the sea.

As Antonio turned and looked back toward the city of Pompeii, he could still see smoke rising above the horizon. His heart was filled with sadness as he thought about leaving his homeland and the friends he had lost. He never imagined he would abandon the city. He always thought he would stay in Pompeii to become a fisherman and take over his father's boat. That dream had now been altered. He'd become a fisherman and take over his father's boat, but in Marina Grande, not Pompeii.

Watching Antonio from a distance, Sharkman continued to think about his old life and the impact the loss of his wife and children had on him. He walked over to the boy, placed a consoling hand on his shoulder and said, "You will find a good life on this island."

Antonio looked up at the old man and gave him a hug. "I'm scared," he whispered. Now that he knew Sharkman could hear him he wanted to tell the old fisherman how he felt about coming to this strange place.

Nodding, Sharkman returned the hug. Aware that he couldn't continue to talk to Sharkman without the crew and his father becoming suspicious, Antonio ran into the ship's cabin and returned with a large piece of papyrus and a writing tool. He scribbled, "*Quid mihi dices de Capreis insula?* (What can you tell me about the island of Capri?)"

Writing back, Sharkman told Antonio that the island was located in the Tyrrhenian Sea on the south side of the Gulf of Naples and it had a rugged shoreline with high limestone cliffs that were dotted with caves and massive boulders.

Taking the piece of papyrus back, the boy anxiously asked, "*Quod est oppidum de Marina Grande simile?* (What is the town of Marina Grande like?)"

Smiling, Sharkman responded in Latin telling the young man it was a small fishing village with enough deep water to provide a safe harbor for their vessel.

"*In hac insula habitas?* (Did you live on this island?)" Antonio wrote.

Sharkman shook his head no.

"*Ubi habitasti antequam te in aqua Pompeii invenimus?* (Where did you live before we found you in the water off of Pompeii?)"

Sharkman motioned for another piece of papyrus and he wrote, "I lived on a small island a great distance from Capri called Fortune island. The waters around my home were crystal clear and filled with many colorful fish which I caught and sold in a local market twice a week."

Sharkman could tell by the expression on the boy's face that he had a lot more questions. Luckily, Julius interrupted and began shouting to his crew, "Get ready to drop anchor and make your way ashore. We've arrived at Marina Grande."

Nearly all the people from the fishing village had come to the beach to see who the strangers were. Julius was the first person to jump over the side and wade ashore to greet them. After talking to the village elder, Julius waved to his crew and their families. "You can come ashore."

Sharkman was the last to leave the fishing vessel. He was glad he had made it to the safety of Capri but he knew that Baka would soon follow him here. The question was were there any places where he would be safe from the demon and would he ever be able to get back to his own time. By the time he made it ashore, Antonio had explained to the village fishermen that Sharkman was a deaf-mute, so they greeted him with smiles and slaps on the back. Sharkman smiled back at their greetings and nodded in appreciation. However, he knew he wouldn't be staying long. Tonight, when everyone was asleep, he would slip out of the village and find a place to hide in the mountains. There, he would begin to think about finding a village far enough away from the coastal communities where he might escape the attention of Baka.

Crooked Island–Hurricane Aftermath

The hurricane hung over Crooked Island for 36 hours and when it left and tracked north, there was almost nothing left of Landrail and the small villages that were scattered across the island. Many of the people, dazed by the storm's intensity, wandered the streets staring in disbelief at the total destruction the storm rendered to their homes and communities. Their life's work had been swept away in one brief, terrible moment.

When Claude Joseph and his wife and son freed themselves from the bathroom, they looked around and cried. The roof was gone, furniture had been swept onto other people's property, and most of the small mementos they had brought with them from Haiti had disappeared.

The school where Claude was principal and taught several classes looked in slightly better shape but it would take months to repair. As principal, he knew he needed to begin the process as soon as possible but there were more pressing things to attend to. And then there was Simone. He knew she was supposed to be with Reggie and Wendell lobster hunting off Fortune Island, but he had no way of communicating with her to make sure she was safe. Cell phone towers were down and he doubted there were any boats available to search for her and her companions.

Claude rummaged through what was left of their house and found a first aid kit to tend to the cuts and bruises on his family. Neither his house nor the school had running water and there was no electricity in either place. They found their refrigerator a quarter of a mile from the house. Luckily, it still contained a few fruits and vegetables and their canned foods were scattered across the school grounds. They might provide enough food to eat for a little while but it wouldn't sustain them for very long. It was obvious they couldn't stay where they were. A little farther away, he spotted his car partially hidden under some debris. It still seemed to be in working order so he cut away some branches in front of the driver's side door, got in, and turned on the ignition. By some miracle, the automobile started and gave him a flicker of hope. Maybe he and his family could drive to the airport and find out when some supplies were going to be transported to the island. Waving to his wife and son to crawl into the vehicle, they drove down the hill hoping that there wouldn't be too much debris blocking the road. That turned out to be optimistic thinking.

A mile from his house, the road became impassable by several large trees and bushes. Shaking his head in despair, Claude got out of the car and surveyed the situation.

"It looks like we have no choice but to walk to the airport from here," Claude said to his wife when he returned to his vehicle.

Claude's wife frowned and pointed out that the airport was probably a good distance from where they were.

"True," Claude concurred, "but we have no choice except to go there. With no water and little food, we won't survive very long at the house. At least at the airport, they'll be bringing in enough food and water for us to live off of and maybe some tents to live in until we are able to work things out."

"Let's get going then," his wife urged. "I hate the thought of us hiking along this road at night, but it appears we have no other choice."

Ben Jenkins, his wife Emily, and her father were thankful to be alive, but their daughter Amy was so shaken by the experience, she couldn't stop crying. After the storm passed, Ben's family and Emily's father, Wilson Cooper, decided they had no other option but to wade through the mucky mangrove swamp back to Cooper's home. They had no idea what they would find when they got there, but they were pretty sure it wouldn't be good. Mosquitoes and biting flies continued to pester them almost the entire way back. Several times, Emily's shoes were sucked off by the mud and they had to stop and reach into the muck to find them. When they finally made it to the paved road that led to Landrail, they discovered it was nearly impassable. The ocean had covered almost all of it with sand, and numerous trees and brush had been dumped on top of it. Exhausted, they took a few moments to rest on the trunk of a toppled palm tree and make a further assessment of their situation.

"Do you think anyone survived this storm?" Emily asked her father.

"I believe most of dem did. The residents dat live on dis island are a pretty tough lot. Dey've survived some bad storms in de past."

"I'm wondering what chances Wendell and his friends have of surviving this one," Amy asked.

"I suspect dey found a cave ta hide in up in de hills. If dey did, I believe de chances dey survived are pretty good," her grandfather replied.

"I hope so. I'm worried sick about them."

"I'm worried too," Ben said, "and we'll start looking for them as soon as we can. Right now we have to take one step at a time. Our first objective is to get to your grandfather's house and check it out. If it's too badly damaged, we'll go to Landrail's dock to see what efforts are being made to bring in food and medical supplies."

"You're right," Emily sighed. Reaching down, she picked up a sturdy tree branch and used it to support herself as she followed her father and the rest of the family through the piles of debris scattered across the road.

The swirling clouds from the storm had pretty much disappeared when Lewis walked to the front of the cave he and his family had taken refuge in. Debris from the storm was everywhere. For now, there was no sense leaving the place where they had sought safety. Their home had been swallowed up by the ocean and his friend's boat was at the bottom of the bay. Like everyone else, they would soon need more food and water. They had taken some food with them, but it would only last a couple more days. Stepping back into the cave, his wife approached her husband and gave him a hug.

"How long do you think it will be before dey get food and water ta de island?" Lewis's wife asked.

"Not long, maybe a day or ta. I've checked what we brought wid us and der should be enough fer us ta make it until de first shipment is brought in by boat at Landrail. A tree has fallen on our car so we can't use it ta drive ta town. I'll hike down der tomorrow ta check out de site where de mailboat comes in. If it's not ta badly damaged, I'm sure dey will use dat area ta bring in de first shipment of supplies."

"I hope dey can do dat." His wife sighed as she tried not to cry in front of her children.

"Me ta," Lewis agreed. "While we're waiting, we've got a lot ta think about, like how we will get de supplies we need ta build a new home, get a boat ta replace my friend's, buy myself a new one so I can begin fishing again, and most importantly, try ta rescue Reggie and his friends."

Simone Offered to Blackbeard

Japapa bent over and shook Simone's shoulder. "Wake up. You need to put on some decent clothes. I've been informed Blackbeard's coming for a visit sooner than expected and I want you to look your best."

Simone rolled over and stared into Japapa's menacing face.

"Blackbeard's a very important person. I'm sure you'll like him."

"Yeah. I bet I will," Simone laughed. "I'm not sure I want to meet anyone you like." Simone already knew she wanted no part of Blackbeard. She also was aware that since she wouldn't be doing chores this morning it was going to be more difficult for her to escape.

Simone got up and Japapa shoved her into his cabin and showed her a closet full of clothes. "I want you to wash up and find an attractive dress to put on; then meet me outside. My friend and I will be waiting for you."

After cleaning herself with cold water from a bucket, Simone rummaged through the clothes and grumbled to herself. Most of the clothes appeared to have been plundered from Spanish ships the pirates had captured. A few fit and she looked very attractive in one or two. But she decided it would be a big mistake to greet Japapa's "friend" in one of those. Better for her to show up in a dress that would make her appear less desirable. At the back of the closet, she finally found what she wanted, a drab, not too clean house dress. It had no frilly lace around the shoulders and its bottom hem was tattered and covered with dirt. Pleased with her selection, she decided that she still might appear too attractive so she wiped some soot on her face from the base of one of the candle holders on Japapa's desk. Looking into a mirror in the closet, she smiled at her appearance.

Now she looked just right. Opening the cabin door, she curtsied and greeted Japapa's guest with a smile.

When Simone looked into the pirate's eyes she could see the disgust on Blackbeard's face. It was just the kind of reaction she hoped she would generate. Astonished, Blackbeard turned toward Black Caesar and glared at him with rage. "Is this the beautiful wench you wanted to offer me as a gift? This gutter snipe? She is the most disgusting wench I've ever seen."

Realizing she had just made a fool of him, Japapa grabbed Simone by her hair, looked into her eyes, and snarled, "Clean yourself up! I'm giving you fifteen minutes. If you're not done by then, I'll chop you into pieces and feed you to the pigs. As you're aware, they haven't been fed today and I'm sure they're very hungry." At that point, Japapa dragged a defiant Simone into the cabin and cast her onto the floor.

Picking herself up, she washed away the soot, removed her dress, and quickly selected one of the more attractive garments hanging in the closet. She had no choice but to do what Japapa demanded. However, becoming a member of Blackbeard's harem was about as appealing as being fed to the pigs. As she cleaned up and put on a more attractive dress, she continued to think of a way she could escape.

Outside the cabin, Black Caesar apologized to Blackbeard for the way Simone presented herself. "She's a willful young woman and sometimes I have to teach her the error of her ways."

Blackbeard chuckled. "A healthy dose of discipline should be applied to all women, so they understand their place in life. Let's see if she's as beautiful as you say she is when she's cleaned up."

"I believe you will find her to be as attractive as I said you would. I once considered marrying her myself, but she was too ornery for me. Perhaps you can train her."

When Simone came out of the cabin a second time, she appeared in a beautiful white dress with a hem of frilly lace and her face and arms were completely cleaned of soot. "By God you are a beauty," Blackbeard said. "Come closer, girl, so that I can get a better look at you."

Stepping closer to the stout, robust-chested pirate, she almost choked from the stench emanating from his body. The odor of sweat mixed with the smell of rum and gun powder made her want to vomit. Blackbeard lifted her chin up and smiled. "You are an astonishing beauty. I might make you part of my harem. I want to thank you for this charming gift, Black Caesar. I will reward you handsomely for this prize."

"I'm delighted you're pleased with her. I was worried for a moment you wouldn't find her as appealing as I promised. I'm sure she'll become one of the most desirable of the fourteen wives that make up your harem."

"She definitely will." Blackbeard tipped his hat and smiled at Black Caesar. Taking Simone by the hand, the pirate dragged her off the ship to his jolly boat and anxiously looked forward to adding her to his harem.

Saving Simone

"Any sign of Simone," Wendell asked Reggie as they followed the trail outlined on the map they had memorized.

"None."

"This mosquito infested path is hard to deal with," Wendell complained. "How far away from the safe house are we?"

"Judging from de map we studied, it's about a mile from here. Maybe Simone will be able ta meet up wid us der."

"Let's hope," Wendell grumbled. "We can't leave this island without her."

About a half-mile further on, Reggie spotted a group of men in a clearing and motioned Wendell to stop. "What is it?" Wendell asked.

"It's a group of men dat I remember from de ship."

"Maybe they're headed to the safe house. If they are, we could join up with them."

"Maybe. But before we do dat, I'd like to listen ta what dey are talking about," Reggie whispered. Even though the mosquitoes were dreadful, both hunkered down in the bushes and crawled closer to the clearing in order to hear what the pirates were discussing.

"Have the boys made it off the ship yet?" one of the crew members asked as he swatted at several mosquitoes that landed on his face.

"Yes," the young man with a large scar on his face replied. "I watched them as they snuck off ship. They should arrive at the safe house in about half an hour. It should be easy enough for them to find it with the information on the map I passed to Simone."

"Is the girl coming along with them?"

"No, our captain plans to give her to Blackbeard."

"Great; our captain's plan seems to be working out perfectly. Have the slave dealers been invited to the safe house?"

"Yes. They are very anxious to get ahold of the two young men. The plantation owners and the men that own the salt processing plant in Bonaire are in desperate need of more help. Most of the men we sent them last month are in pretty bad shape and the Dutchman in charge of the salt recovery program needs more slaves."

"I heard the Dutch salt mine operators pack their slaves into small huts at night and work them eighteen hour days hauling salt from ponds in temperatures in excess of one hundred degrees," one of the men said.

"Is that true?" the young man with a scar asked.

"Yes," another pirate replied.

"What a way to live. I'm glad I'm not one of those kids. Our captain must really hate them. I wouldn't want to live like that; I'd kill myself."

"I agree," the leader of the group acknowledged. "But we can't concern ourselves with what's going to happen to them. We must carry out our captain's orders. If we fail to do it, we'll walk the plank and be fed to the sharks just like the Spaniards. Let's head for the safe house and make sure the two young men show up."

Wendell and Reggie were stunned by what they had just heard. "What do we do now?" Wendell asked.

"We've got ta get back ta de ship and warn Simone about Japapa's plans."

"Suppose he's already turned her over to Blackbeard?"

"If he has, we'll meet up wid dem on dis trail and try ta rescue her."

Unfortunately, the young men were too late. Watching from behind some bushes, they were shocked to see Blackbeard dragging Simone from the beach. "What are we going to do to rescue her now?" Wendell whispered.

"Good question," Reggie agreed.

Taking a moment to reflect, Wendell narrowed his eyes and said, "How about creating a diversion of some type. We could scream and throw rocks at Blackbeard and when he turns to see who's creating the problem, one of us could swoop in, grab Simone, and run off with her into the woods."

"And who do you suggest should swoop in and grab her?" Reggie asked with a look of suspicion.

"You, of course. You're stronger and faster than I am."

"Hmm, dat's not one of de greatest plans you've ever suggested, but I have ta admit it might work. I must tell you though; I'm not ta excited about de part where I run in and rescue Simone. If Blackbeard doesn't let go of her, I'm toast."

"I agree it's not the greatest idea I've come up with, but if you have an alternative I'm all ears."

"How about we distract him on de wooden bridge?" Reggie suggested. "De bridge is not very stable, and Blackbeard has ta cross it ta reach his house. In addition, I haven't seen anyone hanging around dat bridge who could help him out if something goes wrong wid our plan."

"That does seem like a good idea," Wendell agreed. "But I'm still not sure we're going to be able to distract him on the bridge by throwing rocks. How about one of us goes over to the other side of the bridge and cut the bridge's support ropes while Blackbeard is making his way across with Simone? When the ropes break, the bridge will collapse and the pirate will be tossed into the creek."

"And den what happens ta Simone?" Reggie asked.

"Blackbeard loosens his grip on her and she tumbles into the creek with the pirate. That's when one of us jumps into the water and rescues her. I was thinking that you should be the one that saves her. You swim better than me."

"How thoughtful of you. How is it I'm always de one ta carry out de most difficult part of de plan? All right, I'll rescue

Simone, but you'll have ta cut de ropes on de other side of de bridge."

"But I don't have a knife sharp enough to cut them."

"It's your lucky day. On our way off de ship, I stole one. I think it's sharp enough ta do de job."

"Fine. Give me the knife. I guarantee you this scheme will work better than the last one we came up with."

"I hope so," Reggie said with some uncertainty. "However, if it's going ta work, you need ta take off right now and get situated on de other side of de bridge and make sure you are prepared ta cut de ropes."

After crossing the bridge, Wendell anxiously waited in the bushes for Blackbeard and Simone to show up at the other side of the rope bridge. It had taken longer than he anticipated for them to arrive, and he had begun to wonder if they'd taken a different route. It was Simone's loud complaints that finally attracted his attention.

"Let go of me, you foul-smelling, bearded goat," she shouted. Loud laughter followed as he watched Blackbeard drag Simone toward the bridge. Frustrated with Simone's disparaging comments, the pirate hoisted her over his shoulder and started walking across the bridge.

"*Great.*" Wendell grinned as he watched the pirate and Simone reach the mid-way point on the bridge. Running from his hiding place, he grabbed hold of one of the bridge's ropes and began slicing through it. Reggie was right; the knife was extremely sharp. Within seconds, the knife sliced through the ropes supporting the bridge and Blackbeard and Simone tumbled into the creek as it collapsed. Simone screamed as she found herself plunging into the water and Blackbeard released a plethora of foul curses. Hopefully, Reggie would be able to rescue Simone before Blackbeard spotted him.

Where is Reggie? Wendell wondered. He stood up and shouted, "Reggie!"

"I'm here," Reggie yelled back as he dove into the water alongside Blackbeard and Simone.

Pushing himself out of the mud, Blackbeard wiped the slime from his face and glared down at Reggie. Reaching for his dagger, the pirate swung his blade at Reggie who ducked just in time to avoid having the knife slice across his throat. Skillfully avoiding Blackbeard's knife a second time, Reggie ducked under the water and surfaced several meters down the creek among the mangroves. It was a great place to hide, but how long would it be before the pirate found him.

When Wendell realized Blackbeard was more interested in getting ahold of Reggie than he was with capturing Simone, Wendell climbed down into the creek to assist Simone out of the water.

"Give me your hand," Wendell yelled. Reaching up, Simone took hold of Wendell's arm and staggered up onto the muddy bank of the creek.

"Where's Reggie?" Simone asked after the two of them took off into the bushes and collapsed.

"When I last saw him, he was trying to escape from Blackbeard. My first thought was to rescue you before the pirate realized you were gone."

"I'm glad you did, but we can't abandon Reggie while that beast is chasing him up the creek trying to slice him into pieces."

"I agree, but how can we save him?" Wendell asked.

Time Portal–Escape

Everyone was asleep. Most of the fishermen had temporarily moved in with some of the residents of Marina Grande and it was time for Sharkman to head into the island's interior. *If I'm lucky, I can find a small community and blend in with the local population. It has to be a place where Baka can't find me. After that I have no idea what to do. The situation seems hopeless. I'm stuck in the past with no way of returning to the future, and I'm being pursued by an evil creature who is determined to extract information from me that will prevent mankind from achieving a more beautiful and peaceful path to the future.*

As the old fisherman made his way along a narrow path that led into the hills, he thought about the people he was leaving behind. There was no way he could tell them why he was leaving. He also hated to abandon Antonio and some of the other friends he'd made in the fishing community, but staying with them would put their lives in jeopardy. Baka would eventually torture them to find out where he was.

About a mile inland, the path he was following split in two directions. One path led along the coast, while the other led further inland. He wanted to follow the path that would lead along the coast but knew that would take him to an area where Baka could easily locate him. It was better he take the path that led inland. As he headed in that direction, he heard something sneaking around in the bushes near the trail. Taking cover, he waited to see who was following him. It didn't take long for Sharkman to discover who it was. Reaching out in the darkness, the old man grabbed hold of the person's toga and pulled him into the bushes.

"Antonio! *Quid facis hic*, Antonio? (What are you doing here, Antonio?)" Sharkman whispered.

Continuing the conversation in his native language, Antonio replied, "When I saw you leave the village I wanted to find out where you were going."

"Do you think we can converse in English?" Sharkman asked.

"Yes."

"It wasn't a good idea to follow me. It could get you in a lot of trouble."

"I don't understand. My father and all of his workers respect you for your skills. You could have a good life among us."

"If things were different, I would stay, but I can't. A powerful, evil demon is chasing me and if he finds out where I am he will torture me. He wants information only I can give him and he won't stop chasing me until he gets it."

"Was it the senator in Pompeii that bought you as a slave?"

"Yes."

"He won't find you. My people won't let that happen. Anyway, he probably died when the city was destroyed."

"I doubt the senator died when the city was destroyed."

"What makes you say that?"

"Because the senator's body was possessed by a demon known as Baka and no volcanic eruption or living person can destroy him."

"No one? Not even one of our powerful Roman gods?" Antonio stammered.

"No one. Not even your Roman gods. That's why I don't want anyone to follow me. If they did, their lives would be in danger. This demon wouldn't hesitate to kill you if it thought by doing so he could get the information he wants from me. Baka is after something I learned when I was fighting as a soldier in a war."

"You were a soldier? What war did you fight in?" Antonio asked.

"In a war that hasn't happened yet. It was called the Vietnam War and took place in a country very far away."

"A war that hasn't happened yet!?" an astonished Antonio replied. "How can that be? Did our gods take you there?"

"No, I actually come from a time and place way in the future. It is very different from the time you live in. In my country, we travel great distances through the air and have sent people to the moon."

"Travel through the air! And your people have been to the moon?!!" Sitting down on a rock, an amazed Antonio just shook his head. "You must come from a very powerful empire."

"I do, but not powerful enough to protect me from the demon, Baka. He has cast me back into your time to punish me and hopefully get the information he wants. That is how I wound up in the water off of Pompeii."

"And that is how you knew what was going to happen to our city?"

"Yes. People from my time weren't exactly sure when the destruction of your city would take place but they suspected it occurred sometime after the 23rd of August of this year.

After mulling over all the things Sharkman had said, Antonio stood up and said, "I want to go with you. I could learn a lot from you and I could help you find a safe place to live."

Looking into the eyes of the young man, Sharkman smiled, thought about the son he'd lost, and wondered if he would have turned out to be as brave as Antonio. He certainly hoped he would have. "I really appreciate your willingness to help, but I can't let you come with me. It's too dangerous. If the demon finds me, he will kill you. He'll have no use for you and will have no reason to keep you alive."

"I'm not afraid of your demon. Between the two of us, we can overpower him and send him back to the underworld where he belongs."

"Well, I'm afraid of him," Sharkman admitted. "With one flick of his finger he could turn you into a ball of fire and you'd become a smoldering cinder. I wouldn't want that to happen to a young man I admire. Just think of the grief your father would feel when he found your body in that condition. For your own safety and that of your family, I implore you to go back to the village and become the great fisherman your father wants you to be."

Saddened by the old man's refusal to take him on his journey, Antonio turned and slowly started down the wooded trail back to the village. Tears filled his eyes when he thought about all the things he could have learned from Sharkman if he had been able to travel with him. And then he began to think about the future world the old man described—*people flying through the air and landing on the moon. I have to see these things for myself.* Turning around, he raced after Sharkman and hoped that he would catch up with him before he disappeared.

Just as Antonio caught up with the old man, a bright light lit up the night sky and the ground began to shake. Was the demon coming to get the fisherman? To play it safe, Antonio hid behind a tree to see what was happening. To his amazement, an old woman stepped out of a ball of light and onto the trail.

"It's time to go," she said to the old man.

Sharkman smiled at the old woman and headed toward the light. "It took you long enough. I thought I'd never escape this place."

"You're lucky I made it at all," Mama Atabei said. "The Seer had difficulty creating this portal in time so we could transport you back to Fortune Island. Now, he is trying to create a second window in time so we can save Wendell, Reggie and Simone."

"Who is this Seer that enabled you to travel through time and rescue me?" Sharkman asked.

"He's a powerful wizard, one who is capable of overcoming the evil Baka."

"Thank God you found him," the old man responded as he stepped into the light and followed Mama Atabei.

Antonio continued to have difficulty understanding what Sharkman and the old woman were talking about but he was determined to follow them. Running from behind the trees, Antonio jumped into the beam of light just as Sharkman and the old woman were swept into a river of light.

As Antonio jumped into the time portal, he was embraced by ribbons of colorful lights. It was like he was swimming in a rainbow. Then the portal of light closed and he was swallowed by pitch blackness. There was no up or down. Flailing his arms and legs, he tried to find something to hold onto. But there was nothing to grab hold of. Suddenly, a pin prick of light appeared in front of him and he found himself being swept toward it. The next thing he knew, he was dumped on to the ground where he spotted Sharkman talking to a wrinkled old man and the old woman he saw him with outside Marina Grande. The old man was sitting on a rock with a wooden staff in his hand and a dissatisfied look on his face. Both the old woman and the man seemed very upset and they were talking to Sharkman in English. When Sharkman spotted Antonio, he stopped talking with the others and walked over to him. "What are you doing here? Didn't I tell you it wasn't safe for you to follow me?"

"I know you told me to go back to the village, and I was on my way to do that. But then I heard voices coming from behind me and I decided to go back and make sure you hadn't encountered the demon that was after you. When I saw the beam of light appear and you and the old woman walk into it, I couldn't resist joining you, especially after what you told me about all the exciting things that will happen in the future. I hope I haven't caused any problems."

"Unfortunately, you have," a frustrated Sharkman replied.

"I'm sorry. Is there anything I can do to make things better for you?"

"No. I'm afraid not. It's too late for you to undo what was done."

"Do you have any idea where we are?" Antonio asked.

"Regrettably, I don't." Sharkman sighed. "I know we're not where we are supposed to be. I think it's time you met my companions. They're not demons but folks that came to Capri to rescue me."

Walking over to where Mama Atabei and The Seer were still having a heated conversation, Sharkman stopped and introduced Antonio. "Just to let you know, he is most comfortable speaking Latin, so if either one of you are fluent in that language, I suggest you use it to converse with him."

"I'm quite fluent in Latin," The Seer said. "I've learned a number of languages during my travels. Let me talk to the young man and see if I can't help him understand what's happened and how he might be able to help us resolve our problem."

"Good," Sharkman replied. "Right now, he's so terrified by what's happened, anything you could tell him to help understand our problem would be good."

Mama Atabei wasn't sure that would work. "The question is will he be able to comprehend what The Seer is about to tell him? Antonio comes from a very ancient society that has no concept of time travel, nor the existence of rockets and flying machines. He'll also have a hard time believing that we come from a place that exists 2,000 years in the future. Even more, he doesn't have a clue that he lives on a round planet that is part of a solar system that exists in a galaxy that spirals around with billions of others as part of an infinite universe."

"I agree," Sharkman replied. "But if we are to undo the mess we're in, we are going to have to teach him. The longer I stay here, the better Baka's chances of finding us."

"*Veni. Sede super petram iuxta me.* (Come. Sit on the rock next to me.) *Ubi habitas?* (Where do you live?)" The Seer asked the young man in Latin.

Continuing in Latin, Antonio replied, "I used to live in Pompeii, but father and I just moved into a small village in Capri when Pompeii was destroyed by a volcanic eruption."

"I know all about Pompeii's destruction," The Seer acknowledged. "But you will like the island of Capri much better. I've been to it many times. I know you are frightened right now and are wondering how you got to this place."

"I am," Antonio admitted. "But how do you know about Pompeii? Did you see what happened?"

"I know everything there is to know about Pompeii and I have seen its destruction take place many times."

"How could you see the destruction of Pompeii take place many times?" a puzzled Antonio asked. "It appears you're blind, just like my grandfather. It's impossible for you to see anything."

The Seer smiled. "I wasn't always blind. Once, I could see as well as you. But as I grew older, I lost my sight just like your grandfather. I was young when I first watched Pompeii be destroyed. I had also visited the city many times before its destruction, when it was a thriving community."

"But that still doesn't explain how you were able to see the destruction of Pompeii take place many times."

After pausing a moment to think about his answer, The Seer realized it had to be in a form that the boy would understand. An explanation using the idea of computers and television wouldn't work. However, telling him a story that involved Roman gods might.

"One day, a very long time ago, your Roman gods came to me and offered me the gift of being able to travel through time. I was to use this gift to learn everything I could about the world I lived in and to use what I learned to help people. They also asked me to periodically visit them and describe some of the things I observed.

During my travels, I visited different places more than once and I informed the gods of my observations. This is how I saw Pompeii's destruction take place several times. Recently, I discovered from my friend, Mama Atabei, that Sharkman and his friends needed help. She told me that a powerful demon called Baka wanted to torture Sharkman to get information about a temple that is located in a jungle. It appears this temple, which is very far away from here, is sacred to our gods, and if Baka finds it, he intends to destroy it. Sharkman and I can't let that happen. And you wouldn't want it to happen either. If the demon Baka destroys it, terrible things will happen to mankind."

Shocked by what the old man had told him, Antonio shook his head in amazement. Initially, he didn't know what to say. Finally, he stammered, "Y-you talk to our gods, travel through time, and are now trying to escape from a demon called Baka who wants to kill Sharkman and all of mankind?"

"Yes. I know it's a lot for you to understand. But it is important that you do, so we can solve the problem you've created when you walked into the light."

"So where are we now? In the past or the future?" Antonio asked.

"I'm afraid to say we're in the very distant past. In this time period, Pompeii doesn't exist. If my projections are correct, we are on land that will become the island of Capri in about 110 million years from now, and we are in serious trouble. Very large and dangerous creatures live here. Even many of the plants that you see around you are poisonous to humans."

"One hundred and ten million years ago? Large, dangerous creatures and poisonous plants?" Antonio gasped. "Why did you bring Sharkman here?"

"It wasn't my intention, but when you stepped through the lit door I call a portal, it changed the path in time I was hoping we could travel along. Now, instead of being brought to the future, we were transported deeper into the past."

"How do you expect to escape from a place like this?" Antonio asked. "Will our gods help you? This doesn't appear to be a place where any of us can survive for very long."

"I'm afraid your gods won't be able to help. It will be up to me and Mama Atabei to figure out a way to get us out of here. To do that, I'll need to create another path in time, one in which you will temporarily travel with us to an island that exists in the future."

Just as The Seer finished talking to Antonio, there was a loud roar from the forest and the ground beneath their feet began to tremble. Looking up, the group watched a large flesh-eating dinosaur exit the jungle and peer down at the group of tasty looking morsels.

"I think it's time to leave!" Sharkman yelled as he grabbed hold of Antonio, and Mama Atabei took hold of The Seer and followed. "There are some boulders a few yards in front us," Sharkman yelled. "If we can squeeze in amongst them, we can hide and avoid becoming dinner for that monster." As they raced for shelter, Sharkman prayed that they would reach it in time. *If the dinosaur devours The Seer and Mama Atabei, neither Antonio nor myself is ever going to make it back home.*

Looking up at the saliva-dripping, tooth-filled jaws of the dinosaur, Sharkman and the rest of his group pressed themselves as tightly as they could between the boulders. It wouldn't be long before the creature's thrashing would cause more rocks to tumble down from the top of the cliff they were next to. If this occurred, they would be buried alive. Nervously looking over at The Seer, Sharkman asked, "Have you been able to open the portal that will transfer us to Fortune Island?"

"Not yet," the frustrated seer replied. "The boy's presence has rearranged the pathways we can travel through and there aren't many of them left for me to work with."

"Does it matter which pathway we take?" Mama Atabei cringed as more rocks tumbled from above. "Better for us to escape to a safer place and live another day than be devoured by this beast or crushed beneath these boulders."

"I agree, but I can't just select any time and place. One mistake and I could wind up taking us to the North Pole during the last ice age."

"Great," Mama Atabei grumbled. "Nevertheless, I suggest you find a pathway soon or we'll wind up becoming dinner for a salivating lizard."

"What's that?" Antonio yelled.

"Where?" Sharkman shouted.

"Up there!" the boy said pointing to the top of the cliff.

It didn't take long for Sharkman and Mama Atabei to discover what the young man was so excited about. A gigantic anaconda was about to slither down between the rocks and devour them for dinner.

Fortunately, the dinosaur saw the snake slithering between the rocks first and seized the creature's head in its powerful jaws. Within seconds, the snake retaliated by wrapping its body around the dinosaur. As the two fought to the death, the ground shook beneath Sharkman and his companions, and more boulders began to tumble down toward them.

"We can't stay here much longer," Sharkman shouted. "While those two creatures are distracted with one another, we should look for a better place to hide."

"That won't be necessary," The Seer said. "I've opened another portal with a pathway that will take us to a safer place." With a wave of The Seer's hand, another brightly lit door appeared in front of them and all four jumped through it just before being crushed by cascading rocks.

Swept through a tunnel of glimmering multicolored light, they landed with loud thuds on the deck of an enormous ship just as a jet plane took off over their heads. Terrified, Antonio placed his hands over his ears and stared at Sharkman in shock. "Was that one of the demons that's after you?" he asked as he watched a jet plane disappear into the clouds.

Japapa and Baka

Baka was furious. Just as he was about to capture Sharkman on Capri, he was rescued by that meddling old woman, Mama Atabei. But there was still a chance he could capture the old man, learn the secret of the temple's location, and then get rid of both him and Mama Atabei at the same time.

Unfortunately, by leaping into the time portal, the boy, Antonio, made the time stream unstable and now Baka couldn't tell exactly where they were headed. His best guess was that Mama Atabei was trying to take Sharkman back to Fortune Island. He would just have to meet up with them later. Meanwhile, it was time to pay Japapa a visit and see how his plans were going with the youngsters.

Japapa smiled when Simone was dragged off by Blackbeard. The girl was more trouble than she was worth. Right now, he needed a drink of rum to celebrate getting rid of her. Stepping into Black Caesar's cabin, he quickly recognized the pervasive odor of sulfur and saw the satanic form of Baka resting in the corner of the room with his feet up on his desk.

"Pleased with the way things are going?" Baka asked.

"Yes. I was hoping to drink some rum to celebrate my success, but I gather you have something more important to discuss."

"How insightful of you." Removing his goat-like feet and hairy lower legs from Black Caesar's desk, Baka stood up and approached Japapa. "I have to admit you look good for a human who's spent the last year in a boiling cauldron of hot tar in Hell."

"Sorry to disappoint you," Japapa snarled.

"Oh no, I'm not displeased with you. I'm quite happy with how you've taken care of the teens. If your plan is successful, all three will be miserable for the rest of their short lives. I just wanted to alert you that there are a few details you should be concerned about."

"And they are?" Japapa asked while removing a handkerchief from his pocket and placing it over his nose to block the stench coming from Baka's body.

"That dreadful priestess, Mama Atabei, rescued Sharkman and now she intends to save the teens." Baka hissed and licked his forked tongue across his demonic face.

"But you told me she can't travel through time to rescue the youngsters, so how can she do anything to upset my plans here?"

"I regret to say that's no longer the case. I've learned through my minions that she has enlisted the help of a magician called The Seer. Through his magical powers he has created a pathway in time that allowed her to go back in time and save Sharkman, and she now intends to travel to this time and rescue the youths and bring them all back to Fortune Island."

"Can't you stop her and this voodoo magician from doing this?" Japapa asked.

"I think I can. But it will be difficult. I'm only able to see Mama Atabei and the others when they've arrived at a certain location in time. I can't see them when they're traveling through the time portal. Initially, I thought they would travel first to Fortune Island and drop Sharkman off. But that's not happening. For some reason they have landed in the prehistoric past and are about to be devoured by a flesh-eating dinosaur. Nothing would make me happier than to see that beast eat them, but I can't let that happen until I find out the location of an ancient temple from the old man. I've been trying to get this information for years but every time I get close, the old man slips my grasp. As you know, this is a difficult bunch to capture and they could very well escape from their present situation and wind up here. If that happens, I want you to alert me of their arrival and I'll try to capture Sharkman and try to get the location of the temple. Should his friends help him slip away from me, I want you to capture the old man and extract the location of the temple from him."

"So let me get this straight. If Sharkman escapes from you again and shows up here, you want me to forget alerting you, capture him myself, and find out the location of this temple."

"Your insight sometimes astounds me," Baka responded sarcastically. "That is exactly what I want you to do."

"Thanks for having such faith in me," Japapa snarled. "So this time you're asking me to succeed at something you've repeatedly failed at? I just hope my skills live up to your expectations," Japapa growled as the demon's satanic form slowly faded from the cabin. Finishing off the jug of rum to settle his nerves, the voodoo priest placed his feet up on his desk and thought about what Baka would do to him if he failed to accomplish this task.

Arrival on an Aircraft Carrier

"Can someone tell me who those strangers on the deck of my aircraft carrier are?" the captain shouted.

"I have no idea, sir," the ship's second in command replied. "I'm having them rounded up as we speak. We should know who they are as soon as I get them below deck and start to interrogate them."

"Good. I want to know what you find out as soon as possible. I can't have strangers walking around on our deck when we are in the middle of an important military mission."

Within minutes of being deposited on the deck of the ship, Sharkman and the others were taken below deck and locked in an interrogation room. "I don't think this is exactly where you wanted us to wind up," Sharkman said to The Seer.

"I can't deny that. But it's better than being crushed by boulders or winding up in the stomach of a large snake," he responded.

"I have to agree with that," Sharkman said while shaking his head.

"What is this place?" Antonio asked with curiosity.

"It's a warship. The people in my time call it an aircraft carrier. It sends planes into the air to shoot down other planes or drop bombs on our enemies. The plane you thought was a demon when we arrived was a jet being sent off on a bombing mission. It's an aircraft that can travel faster than the speed of sound."

"That's incredible. Wow! Have you ever flown in one of these planes?"

"Yes, but not to shoot down other planes or drop bombs on the enemy. We also use planes to travel from one place to another."

"How far can they travel?"

"Thousands of miles."

"That seems impossible! Will my people eventually be able to build planes like these?"

"No. Unfortunately, your people will be attacked by invaders from the North before you are able to build any planes. The good news is that the invasion won't happen in your lifetime."

"I'm happy to hear that. Maybe I can prevent that from happening when I return home."

"Maybe, but it's not likely," Sharkman noted sadly.

"Everyone on this ship speaks the same language as you. Do they all come from the same place?" Antonio asked.

"Yes. I was born in a country called the United States of America. Mama Atabei and The Seer come from a different place. It's an island called Haiti."

"And is the place where you were born very large?"

"Yes, but I no longer live there. Many years ago, I moved away from my birthplace to a more peaceful home on an island in a country called The Bahamas."

Before Antonio could ask any more questions, two officers entered the room and invited Sharkman and the rest of his group to sit down at a large wooden table. After everyone was situated, Sharkman introduced himself and the others by name.

"As you might imagine, we have a lot of questions to ask the four of you," one of the officers said as he turned on a tape recorder he had brought along with him.

"I thought you might," Sharkman said and smiled. "However, I think you're going to find it very difficult to believe anything we have to say."

"Perhaps. Why don't you begin by telling us how you got on board this ship."

"You would begin with that question. It is one of the more difficult ones to answer, but I'll try my best."

"Please do. At the request of the captain, I will be recording this meeting. I hope you understand my need to do this."

"I do," Sharkman replied.

Sitting across from the old man, the commander leaned forward and stared into Sharkman's eyes.

Clearing his throat, Sharkman paused for a moment while he tried to figure out what to say. There was no sense telling them the truth. The commander would definitely not believe him. But he might be able to buy the group some time with a story that would seem a tiny bit plausible. If this works, it might give The Seer enough time to get them out of their predicament and transport them to another location.

"Over the last several days, three of us have been visiting the island of Capri," Sharkman began. "We went there on one of those all-expense paid tours we'd both won in a contest. The tour was paid for by a real estate company who hoped to sell us a condominium during the outing. The old woman, Mama Atabei, and I are friends, and when we were told we'd won the same trip, we thought it would be fun to take advantage of the offer. Mama Atabei, however, refused to go unless she could bring her brother along. He's blind and she was afraid to leave him home alone. Since I didn't want her to miss the trip, I got one of my friends to pay for her brother's fare. Neither of us, of course, were interested in buying any property so, after the real estate people finished giving us a tour of their condos on the island, we told them we were not interested in their offer and took a tour of the city."

The next day, we told the agent that Mama Atabei's brother had become ill and we wanted our return tickets so we could go back to the United States with him. But the agent refused to give them to us.

"I reminded him our prize covered a round-trip. but he told us it didn't.

"After much arguing, he insisted if we expected to return home, we'd have to find a way to pay our own fare back to the United States. Since we had paid for Mama Atabei's brother's ticket, we figured there would be no problem making arrangements for his flight, but Mama Atabei didn't want her brother to go home alone so we looked for another travel agent who would provide us with a cheaper passage to the United States. After a couple of unsuccessful tries, we met up with Antonio who said he knew of an agent that would sell us cheap cruise trip tickets. That afternoon we bought our tickets which included one for the boy.

"We have no idea how we boarded your ship by mistake, and we are all very sorry, about the inconvenience we have caused you. We also hope you realize that none of us intend to do anything that would harm your vessel or its crew."

"I see," the commander frowned and gave a thoughtful nod. "I have to agree with you about one thing. It's very difficult for me to believe anything you've told me. First, it would have been impossible for you to have boarded our vessel since it isn't anchored anywhere near Capri. Secondly, where did you get the togas and sandals you and the young man are wearing? In a hobby shop? Finally, I find it hard to believe that a boy that only speaks Latin managed to hook up with the three of you. So before we continue this absurd conversation, I'm going to fingerprint each of you and talk to you separately to see if I can sort out this whole mess. I can't go to the captain with this crazy story. He would be a lot more confident you're not a threat to this ship and its mission if he knows the truth."

The Cave

It didn't take Blackbeard too long to find Reggie. Grabbing hold of the young man, he pulled him out of the mangroves and attempted to stab him. Once again the pirate missed and the knife struck a tree trunk close to Reggie's head. Looking up in astonishment, Reggie was shocked to find Blackbeard still standing over him with a scowl on his face.

"Too bad I missed," the pirate growled, "but that won't happen again."

Before Blackbeard was able to pull his knife out of the tree trunk, Reggie freed himself from the pirate's grasp and scurried into a thick cluster of bushes on the opposite side of the creek.

"Over here," Simone whispered. "It won't take that beast too long to figure out where you are."

Reggie didn't need any further encouragement. Making his way as fast as he could through a thick tangle of vines and tree branches, he joined up with his friends with a sigh of relief.

"Now that plan A has succeeded, what do you suggest for plan B?" Wendell asked sarcastically.

"Why don't we head to the safe house?" Simone suggested.

"Not a good idea," Reggie cautioned. "De safe house was one of Japapa's tricks. He was going ta have de slave owners greet us der. Right now, I don't have any plan B."

"How come I'm not surprised," Wendell grumbled.

"I guess, for now, plan B entails running away as fast as we can and hope dat Blackbeard doesn't catch up wid us."

"I think plan B should be carried out immediately," Simone anxiously whispered. "Blackbeard looks furious, and he's headed this way. Do you have any other ideas where we might go?"

"None. From what I heard when we were aboard Black Caesar's ship, dis island is crawling wid pirates. If Blackbeard sends out word dat he's looking fer us, our goose is cooked. Der's no way we can escape from dese cutthroats."

"Very comforting," Wendell sighed. "What about plan C?"

"Very funny," Reggie shot back at Wendell. "You know as well as I do dat der is no plan C. We should get away from de coast as fast as possible and find some place ta hide inland. If we're lucky, we'll find a cave where we can hang out. While we're der we might be able ta buy enough time ta determine what our next move will be."

It was almost dark when they stumbled across the entrance to a small cave in a lime rock outcropping. Their journey inland had been horrendous. They had to scramble through acacia trees and greenbrier vines whose thorns tore at their clothes and skin, and they were attacked by hordes of blood-sucking insects. Exhausted, they crawled into the cave through a small entrance and collapsed onto its cool lime rock floor.

Although Simone disliked being inside the cave's enclosed environment and was fearful of its resident bat, roach, and rat populations, she was too tired to worry about them, and like Reggie and Wendell, she let sleep overtake her. It wasn't until early morning the next day that she woke up and was greeted by Reggie's excited announcement that he had found a pool of freshwater at the back of the cave. The thought of getting a refreshing bath to soothe their aching wounds encouraged Simone and Wendell to pick themselves up and follow Reggie to the back of the cavern.

After guiding them to the large pool, Reggie pointed and said, "Rainwater. We can drink it and use it ta clean our wounds."

Amazed at the site of clean water, Simone and Wendell quickly bent over and began drinking from the refreshing, cool water and washing their wounds. When they finished, they sat back and began to talk about what they would do next. Their situation looked pretty grim. They couldn't remain in the cave and if they left the cave, a band of pirates would certainly find them and sell them off as slaves, or even worse, bring them to Blackbeard in return for a ransom. After giving their situation further thought, they decided their best chance of survival was to steal a small boat and journey to one of the offshore islands. Even that would be risky. If they were lucky enough to steal a boat and make it to another island, the place might be occupied by Loyalists who wouldn't think twice about capturing them and using them as slaves.

"We could stay in the cave until Blackbeard and Japapa go back out to sea," Wendell suggested. "It's a good place to hide and it's unlikely anyone would find us here. There's plenty of water to drink, some edible plants nearby, and there's always the possibility we could hunt down one of the island's wild animals to eat."

"Dat's workable," Reggie admitted, "but I don't believe Blackbeard and Japapa will stop looking fer us. At some point, dey'd discover where we're hiding and den dey both would take out der revenge on us. When dat happens, I hate ta think about what dey'd do. Stealing a boat ta escape ta another island is also risky, but I'd rather take my chances on an another island den having ta deal wid dos two here."

"Let's do that. I dread the thought of becoming a member of Blackbeard's harem," Simone responded.

After talking further about their options, they finally settled on stealing a boat and heading to a nearby island. As evening approached, the three weary companions set out to find a place where some careless pirates might have pulled their boat ashore and left it unguarded.

Covered with mud and after losing track of Simone, a furious Blackbeard entered the tavern and demanded a drink from the bartender.

"Have a rough night?" one of the drunken pirates asked. When an uproar of laughter followed, Blackbeard turned and glared at the man. Walking toward him, he pulled out his knife, slit the man's throat, and wiped his knife on his pants. "Does anyone else have something to say?" Blackbeard snarled and surveyed the rest of the men in the room. "If not, I'm happy to offer 50 gold doubloons to any man in this room who captures the young woman called Simone and her two male companions."

"How will we know how to recognize them?" one of the pirates asked.

"That's easy," Blackbeard snarled. "My mate should be here any minute to pass out their descriptions. If you can't read, he'll describe them to you. In addition, if you're able to bring them to my ship by tomorrow, I'll pay you an extra 50 doubloons."

"That's quite a reward." One of the pirates laughed while having another swig of ale. "With that kind of money, I'm sure we'll find them by tomorrow."

"Let's hope so," Blackbeard growled. "As for this scum I've just eliminated, I would like one of you to dump his carcass outside, so I can sit down and have a drink. I'm tired of looking at him. I'm sure the land crabs will be grateful to have a little something extra to eat."

Rumors about Blackbeard's reward spread quickly across the island and within an hour Black Caesar's first mate raced up to their captain with the news. "Captain, the wench you gave to Blackbeard has escaped with the two young lads you captured and he's offering a 50 gold doubloon reward for their capture. All of your crew is out looking for them."

Things couldn't have turned out better, Japapa thought to himself after his first mate left. *For that kind of reward, it won't take long for someone to capture the youngsters and turn them over to Blackbeard. By the time Mama Atabei shows up to rescue their scrawny hides, the pirates will have made short work of them. Now, the only thing I have to worry about is Sharkman and his companions. I'm sure I'll find that meddlesome group, obtain the information Baka wants about the temple, and make sure they are no longer a problem.*

This turn of events called for another draft of rum. Reaching across his desk, Japapa uncorked a jug of rum and filled his tankard to the brim. He would sleep well tonight.

Aircraft Carrier–Interrogations

"Have you finished interrogating our guests?" the captain asked.

"Not yet," the ship's commander replied. "I have to tell you though, they are the strangest lot of people I've ever encountered."

"In what way?" the captain inquired while giving his officer a curious look.

"First of all, the boy, Antonio, does not speak or understand English very well. He speaks and reads mostly Latin. Fortunately, one of the sailors aboard our ship can speak and understand Latin. I had him sit down with the interrogator and talk to the young man. One thing he found out is that the boy is terrified of us. He thinks we are some sort of gods who control flying demons that destroy people."

"Interesting. Do you know where the boy comes from?"

"Yes. From Capri. He said he and his family recently moved there from Pompeii. Evidently, they escaped to the island just before a volcano destroyed their city."

"That's strange." The captain scratched his head and took a moment to reflect about what his commander was telling him. "There's been no recent eruption of Vesuvius near Pompeii that I know of."

"I know. It appears the Pompeii he's talking about existed over 2,000 years ago."

"Is the young man mentally challenged?"

"I asked that same question of the interpreter and he said he didn't think so. As far as he could tell, the boy appears to be completely sane."

"And do you feel the same way?"

"I do, but I could have him interviewed by a psychologist if you'd like."

"I might, but that'll have to wait until we get back to port. Did he give you any idea about how he and the others got aboard my ship?"

"He did. But this is when his story gets really bizarre."

"Go ahead. This whole situation has already reached the absurd level. I can't wait to hear what else you have to tell me," the captain groaned and shook his head in disbelief.

"Antonio claims our four visitors have used magic to get aboard our ship. He said he jumped into a bright flash of light when he was following Sharkman on Capri and the next thing he knew he found himself on his hands and knees next to a river running through a tropical jungle. He said the blind man, who he calls 'The Seer', told him that they had just traveled through time and were somewhere in the distant past about 110 million years ago. The old man said the Roman gods had given him the power to travel through time and his plan was to use this power to take Sharkman back to his home in the Bahamas where he would be safe from an evil demon called Baka. Unfortunately, when Antonio stepped into the light, he apparently upset the magician's plans and they went backwards in time rather than forward. According to the boy, while they were on a river bank and The Seer was trying to figure out a way for the four of them to get back to the future, they were nearly killed by a giant dinosaur and an enormous snake Sharkman called an anaconda. Allegedly, The Seer was able to use his magic again to transport them forward in time before the creatures could devour them. However, the magician wasn't able to take them far enough into the future, and as a result, they landed aboard our ship."

Cupping his head between his hands, the captain stared at the table and groaned. "Have you talked to the others?"

"Yes. Neither The Seer or the Haitian woman called Mama Atabei provided much information. They both said they regretted coming aboard our ship and thanked us for our hospitality and the accommodations we provided. The blind man said they all would be leaving very shortly because they had to rescue some youngsters that had been captured by pirates. Mama Atabei said it was important for them to reach the youths soon because their lives were also being threatened by the demon Baka. From what I've been able to determine, the creature they call Baka is the devil and it has formed some sort of alliance with one of the pirates called Black Caesar to get revenge on the youngsters for something they did to him in the future."

"What about the fingerprints?" the captain asked. "Have we gotten back any information on them?"

"Nothing for three of them, but they were useful to help us identify Sharkman. He is an Army lieutenant in Vietnam and his real name is Jeff Mason. The only problem is our records show he's currently a prisoner in North Vietnam and has been there for over a year. They also show he was captured during his last tour while leading a platoon into the jungle. According to his commanding officer's report, he was on a special mission to locate and take charge of a sacred temple that he and his men had discovered on an earlier scouting expedition. All of the men in his platoon were reportedly killed during the mission except Sharkman. Some of the locals indicated he was severely tortured by the North Vietnamese and then taken to a prison camp in North Vietnam. Since then, no one has heard anything about him."

"So you are telling me the fingerprints we have from a person we know as Sharkman actually belong to an Army lieutenant known as Jeff Mason who is approximately 25 years old and is currently in a prison camp in North Vietnam?"

"Yes, sir."

"How old would you say the person we have in our custody is?"

"About 75," the commander responded.

"Did you have someone else check the fingerprints to confirm your initial findings?"

"I knew you would ask, so I had them checked again."

"And?"

"I got back the same results."

"You realize what you're telling me is basically impossible," the captain said and shook his head.

"I do. That's why I think you should interview Sharkman, or whatever his real name is, yourself."

"You're right. This whole thing is incredible but there is no way in hell I can report this incident back to command headquarters. They would think we're crazy and put both of us in a psychiatric institution. Where is the old man right now?"

"In your office. I thought that would be the safest place for you to interview him. I didn't think you would want anyone else overhearing what he might have to say."

"I agree," the captain said and slowly stood up and walked down the ship's passageway to his office.

Failed Escape Attempt

"Does it look like anyone has used the boat recently?" Simone asked Reggie as they watched it from behind a sand dune. Oh, and thank you both for the clothes. They don't fit, but they'll help keep the bugs off."

"No problem," Reggie grinned. "We needed ta get some fer ourselves. When we saw dem hanging on a clothes line, we grabbed dem and ran off as fast as we could. As far as de boat is concerned, it's been sitting on de beach der fer a while. Whoever owns it might be out looking fer us, but it could also be a trap," Reggie admitted. "When Wendell and I scouted out de nearby tavern, we heard a lot of talk about Blackbeard placing a ransom on our heads. He's offering 50 gold doubloons ta anyone who captures us and brings us ta him."

"That's a pretty substantial reward. That means there probably isn't a man on this island who isn't trying to find us," Simone lamented.

"All de more reason ta steal dis boat," Reggie replied. "One thing is certain, we can't stay on dis island. If we do, someone will eventually capture us and we'll be sold as slaves. I fer one, don't look forward ta dat happening."

"So what do you suggest?" Wendell asked.

"We should wait until dis evening and if no one comes back fer de boat, we take off wid it and row ta one of dos islands I've spotted offshore."

"How far do you think we'd have to row to get to the nearest one?" Simone asked.

"My guess is no more dan half a mile and der's plenty of moonlight ta find our way. I also scanned de shoreline and spotted several other small islands ta de south dat would be ideal. Dey are a little farther from shore, but I don't think we'll find anyone living on dem. Dey look ta small ta raise crops on and I doubt dat der is anything on dem dat would interest a pirate."

"I suppose we have no other choice but to head to the nearest one," Wendell acknowledged.

It was shortly after midnight and no one had come to get the boat so the teens proceeded to carry out Reggie's plan. After helping to push the boat into the water, Wendell ran back and searched for a set of the oars the pirates had hidden in the bushes. Waving to his friends that he'd found them, he returned to the boat and they began rowing away from the beach as fast as they could. It was impossible to describe the relief they felt as they watched New Providence fade into the distance. The thought of becoming slaves was frightening. Their parents had told them how their ancestors were captured in Africa and brought to the New World where they were made to work in coal mines and grow cotton. They also told them how many of their people died making the trip across the Atlantic and how many others died working in the fields. For the first time in their lives, they began to have a better understanding of how horrible life was for their ancestors. The fear of torture and being killed increased their anxiety as they frantically rowed toward the island Reggie had spotted earlier.

What will happen to us after we get there? Simone wondered. *How much food and water will we find on the island? And where will we go next? In this world, black people are considered nothing more than animals. Will we find other blacks who have escaped and are hiding out on the islands or will the islands have no human inhabitants at all? Perhaps the biggest question is will we ever be able to return to our own time. And if we do, will the treasure we retrieved from the Spanish galleon still be there and was it worth all the trouble we went through to get it? Greed is a terrible thing; are we fooling ourselves into believing some good will come from all the trials we've endured?*

There were lots of questions with no answers. Over time they might find the answers to some, but for now they would just have to live one day at a time and hope for the best. When the boat finally bumped against a tangle of mangrove roots, Simone looked up and was relieved to see they'd finally reached the small island they were headed for. As she made her way ashore, she hoped she would be able to get some rest and perhaps find some answers to the questions plaguing her.

Japapa's head felt like someone had hit him with sledge hammer. He should never have drunk that last tankard of rum, but he couldn't help celebrating the news he'd received about the reward Blackbeard had offered to find the youngsters. By now, someone had certainly found those rascals and claimed the money. Just thinking about the punishment Blackbeard would inflict upon them almost made his headache go away, but not as fast as he hoped. Gingerly standing up, the room began to spin and the pungent smell of sulfur made him want to vomit.

"Not feeling too well?" Baka asked as he watched Japapa grab hold of the desk next to his bed to steady himself.

"No. I'm not used to drinking a lot of rum. It wasn't something you offered me when I was in Hell."

"That's true," Baka admitted. "I couldn't allow alcohol becoming a problem when you were working so hard to clean out the tar pits."

"You were always so thoughtful that way," Japapa snarled as he wrapped a wet rag around his head. "I'm surprised to see you again so soon. I hope you're here to give me some good news."

"As a matter of fact I am. First of all, I'm happy to report that I've located Simone and her friends. In addition, I'm offering you this gold locket the teens retrieved from a sunken Spanish galleon."

"Where did you find the locket?"

"I retrieved it from the place the teens were hiding their treasure."

"So you mean to tell me that none of the pirates have found them?"

"No. However, with the information I have, it will allow you to capture them and collect the reward yourself. I'm sure Blackbeard will be extremely pleased with your resourcefulness and he may even place you in charge of one of the ships he's recently captured rather than making you an assistant aboard his flagship."

"So where are they?" a curious Japapa asked after he washed his face with a bowl of freshwater and patted it dry with a towel.

"Not far from here. They stole a boat last night and rowed to an island just a short distance off shore."

"I think you'll find the locket I just gave you useful when you search for the teens. It was owned by a voodoo priestess who belonged to a cult that could change themselves into different animal forms to hunt down their victims. By holding the locket tightly in your hand and thinking about the life form you would like to become, the transformation will take place. I believe you will find it very helpful in locating the youngsters."

"Great," Japapa said as his headache slowly began to disappear. Taking hold of the locket, Japapa smiled. "Thanks for telling me about the locket's power. I'll use it to begin the transformation immediately."

"A good idea. But remember what I told you. Sharkman, Mama Atabei and The Seer may show up at any time. I'll try to prevent them from becoming a problem but if I don't, I'll leave it up to you to take care of them, especially Sharkman. So try to get the youths into the hands of Blackbeard as soon as possible. Once he has them, it will be more difficult for that trio to rescue the youngsters."

"Understood," Japapa acknowledged and hastily made preparations to start the transformation process.

"Could you be more specific about which island they're on?"

"If you head west down the beach about a half mile. You'll spot it. It's the first island that you'll see offshore when you head in that direction."

"Thanks," Japapa said as he quickly left his cabin. Getting rid of those youngsters would be an extremely gratifying and profitable experience. The wolf he had become leapt into the water and quietly swam toward the nearby island where the youngsters were hiding.

••• >>> •••

"Did you spot anyone else on the island?" Simone asked when Reggie returned from his scouting expedition.

"I didn't see any people but I did hear a large animal moving around in de bushes. When I went ta see what it was, it turned out to be a wolf. I never heard of wolves living on dese islands so de only thing I can figure out is someone captured one and let it loose. Nevertheless, I don't think we should stay here. Dis place is ta close ta where de pirates anchor der ships and one of der crew is bound ta visit dis island and find us."

"I was hoping you'd come back with better news," Wendell lamented. "Where do you suggest we go?"

"Good question. I don't know how far away de next island is. I think de best thing we can do is ta hide out here until nightfall and den head out ta one of de islands dat's further away and safer dan dis one. While I was gone, I did manage ta spear some fish. If we're going ta row ta another island, we'll need ta eat in order ta keep up our strength."

"I agree you should keep up your strength," Japapa chuckled, "especially if you are going to look your best at the slave market. In the meantime, I would really enjoy having some of your fish," Japapa said as he stepped into the clearing.

"H-how did you find us?" an astounded Simone stammered as she stood up.

"That was easy. Baka has been keeping watch over you ever since he threw you back in time. When he saw you settle on this island last night and heard about the reward Blackbeard was giving for your capture, he immediately reported your whereabouts to me. That was no wild animal you heard moving around in the bushes, it was me in the form of a wolf listening to your plans.

"Since Baka was so grateful for all the help I had given him, he gave me this gold locket as a gift." He lifted the locket out of pocket and showed it to Simone. When she saw it, her body began to shake and she cried out in fear.

"I see you understand what extraordinary powers the locket gives me. In addition to the locket, Baka also expects Blackbeard to make me master of one of his ships."

"Lucky you." A terrified Simone shivered and stepped back from the evil priest.

"Now, now, my dear." Japapa smirked and placed a hand on the young woman's shoulder. "You can't win all the time. Just think of how happy Blackbeard will be to see you and, for a while at least, he will make you one of his most prized possessions."

"Lucky me," Simone grumbled. "I can't think of a better way of spending the rest of my life."

"I knew you'd feel that way," Japapa grinned. "I told my men where I was going. As a matter of fact, I see them coming now. Turning to his men as they came ashore, he said, "Tie the trio up and take them to Blackbeard's house."

Crooked Island Restoration

A couple of weeks had passed and things were beginning to return to normal on Crooked Island, but there was still no word about what had happened to Simone and the boys. Seated together in the Landrail restaurant, the families discussed the impact of the hurricane and how they planned to deal with its aftermath and find the youngsters.

"The school had been severely damaged," Claude Joseph informed the group, "but the government has already shipped supplies to repair it and we're about to start replacing the roof on our house."

Emily Jenkins added, "My father's home was completely destroyed and most of the debris from it washed out to sea. Residents found pieces of it hundreds of miles away. Parts of it were washed up on Long Island and the Acklins. After Ben, my father and our daughter and I cleared away the remaining debris," Emily added, "we saw that the foundation of Dad's house was still there and in good shape. We've ordered the supplies to rebuild. It will take six months at least to complete the job, but we've gotten some neighbors to agree to help Dad with its construction. Ben and I have to return to work in New York but we'll come back as often as we can to help. Dad's going to stay with our cousin in Colonel Hill while the reconstruction is going on and our cousin offered to help my father look for the teens while we are away."

Lewis Sands' home had also been completely destroyed and he and his neighbors had helped each other clear their properties. "Like de Jenkins, I've ordered supplies ta rebuild, but I'm told it will take a few more weeks fer de materials we need ta reach Landrail," Lewis noted. "In de meantime, my family and I are certainly grateful fer de government tents. De living conditions dey provide aren't ideal but dey'll do until we get back ta normal."

"Has anyone found out what has happened to the youngsters?" Ben asked Lewis Sands.

"Not yet," Lewis replied. "Dey've sent drones over de islands ta look fer people over de last couple of days and dey've found quite a few residents stranded by de storm but no sign of de teens. I'm sure dey're still alive. Reggie is pretty smart. Der are lots of caves where dey could have taken shelter. I'm certain dey'll show up soon."

"I heard they found what was left of your boat drifting off Fortune Island," Claude said.

"Dey did. It was pretty beat up. If I can't repair it, I'll have ta buy a new one. De kids apparently anchored it off Fortune Island and it broke free during de storm. I had what was left of it towed ta de dock at Landrail yesterday. Der's still de matter of replacing my friend's boat dat I had out fishing when de storm hit. I wish now I hadn't borrowed it but I loaned my boat ta de kids and it turned out ta be such a beautiful day, I couldn't resist going fishing. I have some money ta pay fer a new one, but I'll have ta borrow de rest from de bank ta buy one ta replace his."

"We have enough money to help you out," Emily said. "There's no need for you to borrow more money from the bank."

"Thanks. Dat's very generous of you. I'll pay you back as soon I can."

"There's no need to do that either," Ben replied. "We consider you a friend. I just hope they find our youngsters soon."

Nodding in agreement, the group began to eat lunch, each of them hoping they wouldn't have to wait too long to see the smiling faces of their children.

Aircraft Carrier–More Questions

When the captain entered his office, Sharkman stood up and offered to shake his hand but the officer didn't seem interested in reciprocating.

"Please sit down," he said abruptly. "Before we start, I would like to know your real name."

"As far as I can remember people have always called me Sharkman. It was a name I acquired in the Bahamas when I became a shark fisherman. A lot of the locals also thought my facial features reminded them of a shark. I suppose my parents gave me another name but I've no memory of what it was. To tell the truth, I've been called Sharkman for so long I can't remember the legal name my parents gave me. Unfortunately,

GARY SCHMELZ

both my parents died when I was young and I had to move in with my aunt when I was about four years old."

"I see. And you don't recollect having any other name? Certainly your aunt and uncle called you by some other name and they must have had a copy of your birth certificate."

"I guess they did. But they never showed me a copy."

"When I went to school everybody called me Jeff."

"Then how did you get your driver's license?"

"I used my uncle's last name, 'Johnson' together with the first name everybody called me in school.

"And when you were drafted, you used these names as well?"

"I guess." Sharkman shrugged his shoulders and stared back at the officer.

"And what would you say if I told you that your fingerprints belong to a man called Jeff Mason? I got them from your military records."

After giving the captain a quizzical look, Sharkman said, "I guess it's possible my name is Jeff Mason. As I said, I was very young when my parents died and I only remember my aunt and uncle calling me by my first name, Jeff."

Nodding his head, the captain attempted another line of questioning to see if he could be more successful. "If you don't mind my asking, how old are you?"

"Seventy-five maybe 76—I'm not quite sure. I ran away from my aunt and uncle's place when I was a teenager."

"Then you didn't join the military as the documents I have in my hand suggest?"

"Definitely not. I hated what the war represented."

Tapping his index finger against his desk, the captain began to lose his patience. "Do you ever tell the truth?" the captain asked.

"Almost always. Of course like most kids, I did fib to my aunt and uncle on occasion to avoid getting into trouble."

Exasperated, the captain glared at Sharkman, and took a moment to study the man. He was obviously lying about everything—but why? Was he giving the old man they called The Seer time to figure out a way for them to escape? As unlikely as that seemed, he suspected that it was exactly what the old fisherman was up to. The crazy thing was that he was beginning to think that they might be able to pull it off.

"Why are you stalling?" the captain asked. "Since nothing you have told me so far is true, the only conclusion I can reach is that you're buying time so The Seer can figure out a way for you to escape. The fingerprints we took from you definitely show that you are Jeff Mason. The only problem is Jeff Mason has been in prison in North Vietnam for over year. He was captured while he was on patrol attempting to lead a platoon of soldiers and the local leader to a temple in the jungle. Our records also show that he is only 25 years old."

When the captain showed Sharkman copies of the military records that had been sent to him, Sharkman gave the captain a look of surprise. "How can that be? It's obvious that a person can't be in two different places at the same time. The military must have made a mistake."

"I doubt they did, so why don't we start from the beginning. But this time, you'll begin by telling me the truth. Again, I want you to know I will be recording our interview," the captain announced. "Do you have any objections?"

"No," Sharkman replied and folded his hands in his lap as he sat in front of the captain's desk.

"Good. Let me begin by asking you again. Are you Sergeant Jeff Mason?"

"Since you already have my fingerprints and other pertinent paperwork, it's quite obvious that you already know the answer to that question. But for the purposes of the recorded interview, the answer is yes."

"Finally, the truth. What a relief it is to be getting somewhere in this investigation. I would also like to know if you are the same Sergeant Jeff Mason who is currently being held captive in North Vietnam?"

"Yes and no."

After a short pause the captain said, "I'm not sure I understand your answer."

"I certainly understand the reason for your confusion," Sharkman replied. "To clarify things, I will begin by telling you that I am definitely the same Jeff Mason being held in a prison camp in North Vietnam, but the person you see sitting in front of you is a much older person. To be exact, I am fifty years older than the Jeff Mason being held in prison."

"And exactly how is that possible?" the captain asked and leaned forward with interest to make sure he could understand Sharkman's response.

"Through time travel."

"Let me get this straight. You're telling me you've just journeyed over a hundred million years from prehistoric times to land aboard my ship through time travel, and time travel is the reason the Jeff Mason I'm talking to can be in two different places at the same time?"

"That is correct."

"You realize, of course, that this story is almost as absurd as the last one you told me."

"I do. But as far-fetched as it seems, it's the truth."

"I see."

"It was never my intention nor the intention of the others traveling with me to come aboard your ship. Unfortunately, our journey through time was disrupted when the young man you know as Antonio mistakenly joined us and subsequently changed the time and location we were trying to get to. It is my hope that this problem will soon be rectified and we will be able to leave your ship and complete our journey."

"And your mission is to save your young friends who have been captured by pirates?"

"Yes."

"Well, at least this story agrees with the one the young man gave to my interpreter. It is also my understanding that the teens you are trying to rescue are being threatened by a demon called Baka who is attempting to take revenge on them and you for something that you did to him in the future."

"Yes."

"And that you expect to travel back in time to rescue them before this demon captures them?"

"Yes, and you'll be glad to know my friends and I hope to leave your ship very soon. And when this happens you will probably never see us again, certainly not during this time period or in the immediate future."

"And exactly how do you intend to leave this ship to carry out your mission? Since you are all aware, you are being kept under extremely tight security. There's no way you can just walk away from this ship. Let me take a guess—you intend to escape by stepping through a time portal and traveling back in time?"

"Yes." A smiling Sharkman looked over at the captain and said, "However, I have no idea when this will happen. As I said earlier, I expect it to be soon. I guess the best response I can give you is to say that the process is well above both our pay grades."

It was 0500 hours when Captain Michael Sims watched the last of his jets take off for another bombing run in North Vietnam. It didn't take the planes very long to disappear into the early morning clouds. It was a breathtaking sight, one the captain took great pride in. Now, like the rest of his crew, he would anxiously await their return and pray they all would make it back to his ship.

Stepping down from the bridge he thought about the conversation he'd had the previous day with Sharkman. The old man had told him they would be leaving shortly. In order to prevent that from happening, he had ordered the visitors locked in separate rooms. He wasn't sure that would prevent them from escaping, but it was worth a try. It wasn't until he saw his second in command frantically approach him on the stairwell that he suspected he'd not been successful.

"They're gone," his officer said with an astonished look. "We've searched throughout the ship, but so far we can't find a trace of them."

Smiling, the captain looked over at the commander and told him to discontinue the search.

"But why? They could still be on the ship, and there's no telling what damage they could do."

"I appreciate your concerns, but I don't think you'll find them no matter how hard you look, nor do I believe you'll find they've done any damage to the ship."

"Do you wish me to fill out a report for Pacific Command?"

"No. In all probability, after reading our report about them, they'd relieve us from duty and put us in a mental hospital for observation."

Blackbeard's New Guest

"Stop pulling on my arm, you ugly brute," Simone scowled as she was being dragged to Blackbeard's large living quarters on New Providence.

"Still as feisty as ever," Japapa scowled as he knocked on the wooden door to the pirate's residence.

A slim, attractive, young woman with long, dark hair and flawless facial features responded to their knock. "Come in. Please take a seat in one of the chairs facing the breezeway. You'll be a lot more comfortable there while I let Blackbeard know you've arrived."

When Blackbeard entered the room, Japapa stood up and shook the pirate's hand while Simone remained seated with her arms folded across her chest and glared at the two men.

"I see your companion is not very pleased to be here," Blackbeard chuckled. Walking over to Simone, the pirate smiled and said, "I am so happy to see you've returned to join my harem."

"I have no intention of becoming one of your mistresses," Simone snapped. "You're nothing more than a disgusting cutthroat with an overrated reputation."

"She really is a feisty lass," Blackbeard said as he turned toward Japapa. "I like feisty wenches. I enjoy making them see the errors of their ways. How were you able to capture her and her companions so quickly?"

"One of my crewmen reported that they had seen her escape from your clutches and that you had offered a large reward for the capture of her and the boys. Later, one of my men spotted them stealing a boat and rowing out to a nearby island. The next morning, I rounded up a couple of my crew and captured them before they could look for another place to hide."

"That's a big fat lie," Simone laughed. "You couldn't find a runaway if they were hiding aboard your own ship. If it wasn't for Baka telling you where we had run off to and the use of the locket Baka gave you, you and the rest of your crew would still be looking for us."

"And who exactly is Baka?" Blackbeard asked Japapa suspiciously. "Maybe he's the one I should be giving the ransom money to."

"I haven't a clue what she is talking about," Japapa snarled. "That wretched child is always making up stories. You can't believe how grateful I am that you're taking her and the two young men off my hands. They've been a nuisance ever since they arrived aboard my ship."

"Well I'm glad to say you won't have to put up with them much longer. Here is the reward I promised for their capture. In addition, I'm making you a lieutenant aboard my flagship, the *Queen Anne's Revenge*, where you'll be given a bigger portion of the bounty we obtain from captured Spanish ships. And now, if you'll excuse me, I have other business to attend to."

"Certainly." Japapa smiled, then turned, and left the house. He wasn't happy with being made Blackbeard's lieutenant, but that was something he would have to deal with later.

"Now what?" Simone asked as she continued to glare at Blackbeard.

"Now, I'm going to have one of the members of my harem bathe you. After that, I'll join you in the bedroom."

"Lovely. I hope you are going to bathe yourself. It's hard for me withstand your obnoxious body odor."

"You mean to tell me you don't find me desirable?" Blackbeard laughed.

"I suggest one of the young ladies that is part of your harem blindfold me before you come into the room. The sight and smell of you might cause me to vomit and faint."

"Very funny," Blackbeard chuckled. "The experience might not be as bad as you think." Motioning a member of his household to take Simone away, the pirate then stepped outside his house and asked a couple of his crew to take the two young men Japapa had brought with him and prepare them for the slave auction.

"I want them thoroughly scrubbed and cleaned by the time I put them up for sale. I'm hoping to get a good price for these strapping youngsters. I've been told that there will be a number of wealthy people in the crowd, including the owner of a salt mine from Bonaire and some cotton farmers. They are desperately in need of new slaves to replace the ones they've worked to death. After I clean up, I'll join up with Black Caesar and head over to the auction and see how things turn out."

•••>>>•••

"You seem to be in a good mood," Baka said as Japapa entered his cabin.

"I am." Japapa answered with satisfaction and placed Blackbeard's reward on his desk in front of Baka. "It didn't take long for me to find the teens. With the information you gave me and the locket you provided, it took me less than a day to capture them. Besides the reward, Blackbeard made me lieutenant aboard the *Queen Anne's Revenge*. I was not exactly pleased with the position he offered, but I can talk with him about that later. He's also going to make my ship a part of his fleet."

"Nevertheless, congratulations," Baka said with a smile. "Evidently he was pleased to see that you were able to capture the youngsters so quickly."

"He was."

"Now all you need to do is make sure they don't escape again."

"The youths are not my problem anymore. Blackbeard's now in charge of them. He intends to sell the boys as slaves, and once he does, Mama Atabei and the rest of the time travelers will have a difficult time trying to rescue them."

"Let's hope that's the case; otherwise we will have to deal with them all over again."

"Do you always have to begin the day with unpleasant thoughts? By the way, what is your status with Sharkman?"

"At the moment, he is being held aboard an aircraft carrier in the Pacific along with Mama Atabei and The Seer. They've also picked up a young boy in their travels."

"Well, that appears to be good news. If they have been captured by the military, they won't be able to rescue the youngsters. Who's the young boy that joined them?"

"He's a Roman, the son of a fisherman who lived in Pompeii before it was destroyed. They seem to have picked him up by accident."

"Interesting. Is he any threat to us?"

"Not that I can tell. But I wouldn't count on any of them remaining aboard that aircraft carrier much longer. The question is how soon it will be before they escape and arrive here. The boy's presence seems to have made it difficult for The Seer to control where they are travelling to."

"Good news for us," Japapa acknowledged.

"Before I leave, I must warn you about the locket. Although you will find it to be very useful, if it is used in the wrong way, it has been known to bring harm to its owner."

"I won't allow that to happen."

"Let's hope not." But the worried look on Baka's face as he left, suggested he knew Japapa was not about to follow his advice.

Slave Auction

"A public announcement listing the slaves that are to be sold today has been mounted in the city square," Blackbeard informed Black Caesar as they headed to the town center together. "I am hoping I will find some wealthy buyers for the young men you delivered to me yesterday. I was told that there were cotton farmers and the owner of a salt processing plant on Bonaire that might be interested in purchasing them."

"How much do you think you'll get for the youths?" Black Caesar asked.

"That's hard to say. Hopefully more than enough to pay me back for the reward I gave you for their capture. Last week, two young men about their age were sold for about 100 pounds each, but a lot of factors enter into the purchase price of a slave. The bidders will examine their overall physical condition and whether or not the slave has some valuable skills that the buyer is interested in."

Blackbeard seemed pleased with the size of the crowd that had assembled in the square when he and Japapa arrived. He took particular note of several wealthy cotton plantation owners and a businessman from Bonaire. Salt was a valuable commodity in the New World and not many slaves survived the extraction process. They were given some food and water to live on and at night the slaves were chained together in small huts where they were barely able to move about. Those that were acquired by the plantation owners had a slightly easier life. Although planting and harvesting cotton was hard work, these slave owners would sometimes allow their workers to have some free time in the evenings and would provide them better living conditions than they'd have in Bonaire.

"I understand from some of my crew you don't approve of slave markets," Blackbeard said to Black Caesar as they moved to the front of the crowd.

Caught by surprise, it took Japapa a moment to remember that he was still in possession of Black Caesar's body and he had to be very careful how he responded to that comment. "I don't," he said. "I was once a slave myself and I don't approve of the way they are treated in the New World. I consider the black people that have been brought here my brothers and sisters. Some have come from the very same village I was born in, while others are from neighboring communities. However, I've made an exception in the case of the two trouble makers I've given you. They refused to work aboard my ship and were constantly creating problems. It is my intention to use some of the reward you gave me to purchase a few of the slaves being offered for sale today and let them work as free men aboard my ship."

"An admirable idea. I hope you have enough money to outbid the plantation owners and businessmen that are gathered here."

"I hope so too," Japapa responded although he had no intention of outbidding any of them.

Before the bidding began, the plantation owners and salt mine owners began inspecting the slaves to make sure they were healthy enough to work. Having participated in these events before, they were well aware that the slaves that were being sold often became ill on their journey from Africa and were not worth the price that the auctioneer was demanding.

Chained together with the others that were about to be sold, Wendell watched in fear as each of the men, women and children was examined as if they were pieces of meat. Mouths were pulled open and tongues and teeth looked at closely: legs and arms were studied for fractures, hair was pulled aside and examined for lice, and muscles were checked to make sure the captives could handle the work they would be subjected to.

"They treat us like we're animals," Wendell whispered to Reggie. "It's disgusting."

"Dey think we are animals," Reggie snapped back in anger. "Haven't you read anything about slavery? Dis was how our ancestors were bought and sold. We were cheap labor. Most slave owners didn't care whether we lived or died. Dey were only concerned about how much money dey could make off of us."

"Quiet! This person wants to examine you further," the auctioneer shouted as he unchained Reggie and pushed him toward the mine operator who wanted to check him for any hidden defects.

After satisfying himself that Reggie would be strong enough to work in the salt flats, the Dutch mine owner told the auctioneer that he was particularly impressed with the youth he had just examined. "He'll live at least two more years working on our salt ponds. His companion, on the other hand, looks too scrawny to be of any use to me. Some farmer will probably be able to use him."

"I'm pleased that you feel that way about the boy. When he comes up for sale, I'll make sure you win the bid."

"Thanks," the mine owner said and gave the auctioneer a large tip.

As Japapa and Blackbeard watched the proceedings, the first group of slaves to be auctioned off was a family of four, a woman and her husband plus their two children. The Dutchman from Bonaire acquired the man, while the woman and her children were purchased by one of the cotton plantation owners. Reggie and Wendell were the last to be sold. Reggie was brought to the platform and purchased for 50 pounds by the Dutchman and Wendell for 23 pounds by a plantation owner.

"I didn't get as much for the youths as I was hoping," Blackbeard lamented, "but I've at least recouped most of the reward money I gave you, and your gift of the girl Simone has more than justified my expenditures. I'm looking forward to spending this evening with her."

Walking over to the auctioneer, Blackbeard collected the money he was owed for the sale of Reggie and Wendell and headed back to his house with Japapa by his side. "I see your ship anchored off shore," Blackbeard observed. "I'm looking forward to seeing you in the morning." As the two parted, Japapa thought how well things had turned out. His revenge against the teens was finally complete. Now it was up to Baka to finish dealing with Sharkman, Mama Atabei and The Seer.

"Where are we?" Antonio asked Sharkman as they peered through the underbrush at the slave auction taking place in the town square.

"This is New Providence. It's one of a small group of islands in the New World that we call the Bahamas. If we have reached the correct time period, this place is occupied by bands of ruthless pirates who are selling Africans to plantation owners and salt miners."

"Are your friends here?" Antonio asked.

"Two of them," Mama Atabei replied. "It appears they've already been sold as slaves. Reggie has been loaded aboard a horse drawn cart that is headed to a slave ship anchored offshore. Wendell has been acquired by a plantation owner. Right now, the farmer who purchased him tied our friend's hands behind his back and has sent him to join several other slaves standing near that path leading into the woods."

"Can you save them?" Antonio asked.

"I think so. Wendell will be the easiest to rescue," Sharkman replied. "While the plantation owner settles his bill with the auctioneer, we'll sneak up behind Wendell, cut the ropes around his hands and flee into the woods."

"What about the other slaves? Do you intend to rescue them as well?"

"I'm sad to say we can't," The Seer said. "If we save them, it will alter our timeline further and I will never be able to return Sharkman to Fortune Island. Right now, because of your presence, I'm already having a hard time doing that."

"I'm sorry I messed up your plans. It was never my intention to create these problems."

"We know," Mama Atabei said and gently squeezed the boy's shoulder. "But we're hoping we will soon be able to correct all the problems generated by you and the demon, Baka."

"I don't want to be returned to my own time. I'd much rather stay with Sharkman when he is sent to the future. I could learn a lot from him."

"I understand, but The Seer can't let that happen. Our future very much depends on you being returned to your own world."

A despondent Antonio followed his companions to the trailhead where Wendell was standing around with the other slaves.

"Stay here," Sharkman whispered to The Seer and Mama Atabie as he sneaked behind Wendell and cut the rope binding his hands together.

"Thank God," Wendell groaned as he took off into the bushes with Sharkman and joined the others. "Reggie has been purchased by a mine owner. He intends to cart him off with several others to a ship anchored offshore. If we are going to save him, we need to do it soon. The ship is leaving this afternoon for Bonaire."

"We know," Mama Atabei said. "We watched him being taken away. Do you know where Simone is?"

"She was taken to Blackbeard's house. He intends to make her part of his harem."

"We'll deal with her later," Sharkman said. "We need to get to Reggie first. If they get him aboard that slave ship, it will make our rescue attempt much harder and there is a good chance we'll never see him again."

Reggie's Rescue

When Japapa returned to his ship's cabin, he was greeted by Baka's demonic smile. The demon's hairy, goat-like legs were once again resting across the top of his desk and he was eating from a bowl of fruit.

"I see you made yourself comfortable in my absence," Japapa said with a smirk.

"I did. These fruits your crew left for you are quite delicious. I have nothing comparable to them in Hell. Have the youths been sold as slaves?"

"Yes. Reggie has been purchased by a salt mine operator and Wendell will spend the rest of his life planting and harvesting cotton. It gives me such a gratifying feeling to realize that I will never see those two again. And, how are your efforts going with Sharkman?"

"Ah yes. I've been wanting to talk with you about that. I'm afraid it's not going as well as I hoped. Standing up from behind Japapa's desk, Baka's smile disappeared as he stepped in front of Japapa and grabbed him by the throat. "It seems that you failed me again, you worthless tub of lard."

"What do you mean?" Japapa gasped as the demon's hand tightened around his throat. "The boys have been sold off as slaves and most certainly will die working for their new masters. And Simone has been added to Blackbeard's harem. All you have to do is capture Sharkman. Once you do, you'll find out where the temple is. With all the different methods of torture you can employ, I'm sure you'll discover its location quickly."

"So that's all I have to do," Baka growled as he watched Japapa's eyes begin to bulge out of his head.

"I don't understand," Japapa gasped, terrified that he was about to be choked to death and cast back down to Hell.

"Sharkman and his wretched crew of misfits are now on this island. They have already freed Wendell and are about to rescue Reggie. I assume it was too much for me to expect you or one of your crew to keep an eye on the teenagers until their fates had been sealed. But no, you were so confident that things were taken care of, you never followed up to make sure there was no disruption to your plans. You spent your time buttering up Blackbeard hoping you might receive an even bigger reward from that puffed up toad of a pirate."

Releasing his grip on Japapa's neck, Baka flung him on to the deck and let out a cry of rage. Stunned by what had just happened, Japapa crawled to a corner of his cabin and stared up at the demon's vengeful eyes waiting for the horrible punishment he anticipated the devil was about to inflict upon him.

"Don't worry. I'll give you another chance to redeem yourself. It's too late to prevent Sharkman and the rest of his gang from rescuing Reggie and Wendell, but they won't leave the island without trying to bring Simone back with them to Fortune Island. Go to Blackbeard's house now. Should you reach the house in time, you'll be able to rectify the problem that you have created. After you do, I'll let you stay a free man until the colonists capture you and hang you from the gallows for being a worthless pirate. In the meantime, I'll make sure The Seer and Mama Atabei are thwarted from assisting Sharkman and the boys. After their efforts to save Simone have been prevented, I want you to bring that trio back to me so I can give them the kind of reward they deserve."

"And Simone?" Japapa asked.

"She'll become Blackbeard's problem."

"There's also the problem of The Seer and Mama Atabei."

"I'll take care of them later."

Before Sharkman, Wendell, and Antonio headed to the beach to see if they could free Reggie, Wendell told Mama Atabei and

The Seer approximately where Blackbeard's house was located. Concerned that something might happen to Simone while they were trying to rescue Reggie, Sharkman asked Mama Atabei and The Seer to head for the pirate's house and keep an eye on what was happening. The two agreed and took off while the rest headed toward the beach where the slave ship was anchored. As they approached the ocean, Wendell noticed that Sharkman and Antonio had brought some tools along with them. "Where did you get those?" Wendell asked.

"We arrived here last night, and stole them from the blacksmith's shop," the old man told him. "I suspected they would be useful to break the lock at the back of the cart and pry open Reggie's chains."

"How much further is it to the beach where the mine owners intend to pick up the slaves?" Sharkman asked as they moved quickly toward the shore.

"Not far," Wendell whispered. "Just over the next sand dune."

"Good. Let's stop for a moment. I want to take some time to figure out how we are going to rescue them."

"Stop? We can't do that now!" Wendell said as he gave Sharkman an incredulous look. "We don't have enough time as it is. Right now the people you rescued me from are probably headed this way. If they catch up with us, we won't have enough time to rescue anybody," Wendell cautioned.

"I know that," Sharkman acknowledged, "but if we rush headlong onto the beach to free Reggie without a plan, we might find ourselves in greater danger. Since you know this area a little better than we do, I want you to find out where the cart carrying Reggie is located and how many men are protecting it. Then report back as quickly as possible. Meanwhile, we'll stay out of sight to avoid getting captured by the people you said are looking for us."

Nearly ten minutes passed and Wendell still hadn't returned. *What's taking the boy so long,* Sharkman wondered. Stepping out of the bushes, the old man looked up and down the trail for signs of their pursuers. He didn't see any yet.

"I'm back," Wendell suddenly announced as he slid down to the bottom of the dune and ran into the bushes where his companions were hiding.

"What took you so long?" Sharkman grumbled. "I was beginning to think that one of the pirates had captured you."

"The cart wasn't where I'd heard the pirates say they were bringing it. They took it further down the beach. The good news is that no one is guarding it and the driver is asleep."

"Great. Let's go. You're right about the people pursuing us. I just heard them shouting to one another in the woods and it won't take them much longer to figure out where we are."

"Thank goodness they didn't discover you." Wendell panted as the trio took off.

Sneaking up to the cart, Sharkman waited briefly to see if anyone had shown up since Wendell had scouted the place out. When no one appeared, he jumped onto the cart, gagged the sleeping driver, and motioned Antonio to tie him up. Meanwhile, Wendell waited at the back of the cart for Sharkman's signal to break open the lock with the bolt cutter he had given him. Fortunately, the old lock was rusty and it didn't take a great deal of effort to break it open.

"I thought you'd never get here," Reggie grumbled as Wendell dragged him out of the cart and began prying open the shackles locked around his friend's wrists.

"Very funny," Wendell snapped back. "You're lucky we're able to save you at all."

Once the shackles were pried open, Wendell took hold of his friend's hand and began running off to meet up with Antonio and Sharkman.

"Wait! We can't leave yet," Reggie protested and tugged Wendell's arm.

"Why not?" Wendell replied.

"Dos are our brothers in dat cart. If we don't save dem, dey will die raking up salt."

"We don't have time," Wendell responded. "I wish we could, but if we don't get away now, we'll both be slaving away in the salt mines."

"Well, I'm not going unless we make sure our brothers can escape from de cart."

"Ok," Wendell agreed. "I've left the back of the cart open. You can use Sharkman's tools to break their shackles. When you are finished, you can meet up with the rest of us. We'll be hiding up the beach and will call to you when we see you coming."

After Reggie freed the slaves, he caught up with his companions and indicated to the old man that he needed a moment to rest before racing off to save Simone."

"Who's he?" Reggie pointed to Antonio before they left.

"A friend," Sharkman replied. "There's no time for questions. We need to get going. By the way, what took you so long to get here, Reggie?"

"I wanted to save de other slaves in de cart, so I went back and broke der shackles wid de tools you stole."

"That was admirable but I'm not sure what kind of problems that will create when we travel to the future. Let's hope it won't be a lot. Now, let's take off. We need to rescue Simone. By now, I'm sure Baka knows what we're up to and will have Japapa waiting for us. Hopefully, Mama Atabei and The Seer have figured out a plan to rescue her."

"Let's hope so," Wendell anxiously replied.

"Great! So would one of you please show me the quickest route to Blackbeard's house," Sharkman said. "The faster we rescue Simone, the faster all of us get off of this island."

"I think I can help," Wendell said. "I heard Blackbeard's house is located outside of town on a hill overlooking the bay where the pirates anchor their ships. Apparently, there's a path behind the tavern that leads to it. We could follow it."

"Sounds good," Sharkman replied. "By now Mama Atabei and The Seer must be worried why we haven't shown up."

Escape to Fortune Island

"Sorry it's taken us so long to catch up with you. We had some difficulty finding the house." Bending over, Sharkman panted as he met up with The Seer and Mama Atabei. Have you found a way to rescue Simone?"

"If you mean a way to break into Blackbeard's house and rescue her without someone seeing us, we haven't. Since we left you, the situation has become worse. Japapa has shown up and has informed Blackbeard of our intentions to rescue Simone. It seems Baka became aware of our plans and passed them along to Japapa. As a result, Blackbeard has increased the security around the house and my idea of sneaking into the building through the backdoor is no longer possible."

Taking a moment to think, Sharkman frowned and said, "Maybe there's still a way for us to succeed."

"What do you have in mind?" Mama Atabei asked. Giving Sharkman a quizzical look, she stepped closer to the old man so she could hear what he was about to suggest.

"I'll let Japapa capture me and the boys while we're attempting to break into the house. Once he gets ahold of us, he won't be able to resist dragging us away to show the demon Baka how cunning he is. Meanwhile, Blackbeard will send his extra security forces home because there'll no longer be any threat of Simone being rescued. Then you'll sneak up into Simone's room, Mama Atabei, and have The Seer return Simone, Antonio, and you back to Fortune Island."

"And what happens ta us?" Reggie grumbled. "De demon hates us. It won't take him long ta figure out some horrible way ta take out his revenge on de three of us."

"After bringing Antonio and Mama Atabei to Fortune Island, The Seer will sneak aboard Japapa's ship and rescue the three of us."

"He will?" Reggie shook his head and stared at Sharkman. "I know I'm a little slow, but I'd really like ta hear how you expect dat ta happen."

"It's a bit tricky," Sharkman admitted, "but I believe we can pull it off."

"I'm all ears. De last time we tried ta outsmart Baka, you almost became shark bait and de rest of us nearly suffocated Now you're telling us a blind man is going ta sneak aboard a pirate's ship and save us by transporting us ta de future before Baka and Japapa can find out de location of de temple dat he's been looking fer fer decades. Now I know we're in trouble," Reggie grumbled and shook his head. "From what I've seen, De Seer hasn't been able ta consistently transport people over long time intervals widout delivering dem ta de wrong place and at de wrong time. What guarantee is der dat he would be able ta come back and save us after he transports de others ta Fortune Island?"

"You have to have faith that my plan will work," Sharkman responded.

"I hope so," Reggie moaned.

"Have you spotted Japapa?" Sharkman asked Wendell when he returned from scouting the north side of Blackbeard's house.

"No."

"I'm sure he's somewhere nearby. What about you?" the old man asked when Reggie returned from exploring the other side of the pirate's building.

"Nothing, but I'm sure he and some of his crew are lying low somewhere getting ready ta ambush us when we make our move," Reggie acknowledged.

"Then let's give them a little motivation. We'll head around to the back of the house and make it look like we're trying to rescue Simone by breaking through the rear window. When we do, I'm almost certain one of his crew will spot us and report us to Japapa, who'll make sure he captures us before we get very far."

"Well, I hope dis bizarre plan of yours works. If it doesn't, Baka will turn us into roasted pigs," Reggie groaned.

"I hope it works too. Otherwise, none of us will make it back to our own time, and I'm sure Baka will find a way to punish us that is worse than turning us into roasted pigs."

••• >>> •••

"Have you seen any sign of them?" Japapa asked one of his crew who was hiding behind some bushes along the pathways leading to Blackbeard's house.

"Not yet," the man answered with concern.

"They should be here soon," Japapa grumbled.

Several minutes later an out of breath crewman came running down the pathway. Gasping for air, he pointed to the house. "I spotted them, Captain. They're trying to crawl through the back window of Blackbeard's house."

Japapa was ecstatic. Racing toward the rear of the house with two of his men, he successfully captured Sharkman and the boys before they could crawl into the building. "Finally," Japapa panted. "You really didn't think you could get away with rescuing Simone? Tie them up," he shouted to one of his crew, "and bring them to the ship's cabin." As he returned to the ship with his captives in tow, Japapa smiled to himself and thought about how pleased Baka would be.

"I see you have brought our "friends" back with you," Baka said to Japapa as they entered the ship's cabin. Stepping around the cabin desk, the demon smiled at the trio. "So nice to see you again," he laughed. "Now the question is what will I do with you. Because of all the problems you created, I believe it should be something deliciously painful, don't you? Something I'll enjoy watching throughout eternity."

"I knew you wouldn't let us down," Sharkman quipped. "If for nothing else, you get an 'A' in creative thinking."

"You three are never at a loss for words," Baka snarled. "I have to admire your sassy retorts considering what I have in store for you."

"Thanks," Reggie responded sarcastically. "Don't let us stop you from thinking of special way ta treat us."

Standing on the second-floor balcony of Blackbeard's house, Simone watched the two pirates standing guard in front of the building. *All of my friends' plans for the future have turned out to be a disaster,* Simone reflected. *There will be no gold. Reggie and Wendell have been sold off as slaves and I'm about to become part of Blackbeard's harem. As far as Sharkman is concerned, there is no telling what happened to him. By now, he is probably dead, and both Japapa and Baka are sitting back in Black Caesar's cabin toasting each other with a jug of rum. The best I can hope for is that my family is okay and that they will live a long and prosperous future in the Bahamas.*

"Having a pleasant evening?" Blackbeard asked as he suddenly interrupted Simone's thoughts and entered the room through a side door.

"Not particularly."

"What a shame. I see you haven't put on the night dress I left for you."

"You really didn't expect me to wear it did you?"

As Blackbeard came closer, Simone turned around and glared at him, hatred emanating from her emerald green eyes. "What will happen to my friends now that they have been sold as slaves?"

"Nothing, for the moment."

"'Nothing, for the moment.' What exactly does that mean?"

"Unfortunately, after your friends were purchased, they were rescued by an old fisherman called Sharkman. Apparently, he intended to rescue you too, but Black Caesar and some of his crew have prevented that from happening."

"And where are my friends now?" Simone's look of hatred turned to one of concern.

"Interesting that you should ask. When Black Caesar took them away, I wanted to know the answer to that exact question. He said he was going to take them back to his ship. He apparently has a friend on board who wants to talk to the youths and Sharkman before they decide what to do with them. I believe they'll turn the boys back to the slave owners. As far as the old man is concerned, I think Black Caesar's friend has other plans for him."

"Did Black Caesar say what the friend's name was?"

"He did. If I remember it correctly, it was Baka."

"Baka! Are you sure that was the name he told you?"

"Yes."

"Take me to them! Please. I'll do anything you want if you'll take me to Black Caesar's ship. My friends are in serious trouble. If Baka gets hold of them there is a good chance he will kill them."

"Why should I want to help them?" Blackbeard laughed. "Those youths have been nothing but trouble to me. I have more important things I need to concern myself with. When I return, I expect you to be wearing that night dress I gave you."

She didn't think Blackbeard would agree to let her help her friends, but it was worth a try. Simone picked up the night dress and began to put it on after Blackbeard left. The game was up.

Sitting on the bed in Blackbeard's house, Simone stared at a painting on the wall and thought, *It reminds me of our new home on Crooked Island. Will I ever get back to see my family again?* She doubted it. Instead, she would be trapped back in time where she would become another of Blackbeard's concubines. As she pondered the gruesome life that lay ahead, she suddenly heard someone moving about on the balcony. Thinking it might be one of Blackbeard's pirates, she jumped off the bed and shouted, "Who's there?"

"Friends," Mama Atabei's raspy voice replied, as The Seer, Antonio, and the old woman stepped out from behind the shadows.

"How did you get into the house?" Simone smiled with relief.

"Have you forgotten what extraordinary powers I possess?" the voodoo priestess chuckled. "And I've brought my friends Antonio and The Seer along for help. Sharkman and the boys created a small diversion to help us out. The guards surrounding your room have just taken off to assist Japapa's men. But they won't be gone long, so we must act quickly."

"And who exactly are The Seer and the young boy?" Simone asked as she stared at the blind man and the youth standing next to Mama Atabei.

"They're your salvation," the priestess answered with a smile. "But I don't have time to provide more information about my friends. In a moment, The Seer will open a portal in time. When he does, a bright light will appear and I want you and the young man to step into it. Once you do, I will follow you and we all will be transported back to Fortune Island close to the place and the exact time you left."

"Will The Seer be coming with us?"

"No. Just the three of us will be leaving for the island. I'm afraid the young man doesn't speak English, but if you know any Latin you might be able to communicate with him. Once we arrive on Fortune Island, we'll stay put until The Seer is able to rescue Sharkman and the boys.

"We don't have time to dally; step into the portal of light in front of you. As I'm sure you're aware, Wendell and Reggie are in grave danger. Baka is about to send them to another planet where every life form they come in contact with will either kill them or make them extremely ill. If he succeeds, you will never see your friends again and they will most certainly die of starvation or get devoured by some nasty meat-eating creature."

"What about Sharkman? What will happen to him?"

"Baka will attempt to torture him. He wants to find the location of a temple the old man discovered years ago. It is very important that Sharkman does not reveal the temple's location. If he does, it could bring about the extinction of the human race."

"Are you ready for an experience of a lifetime?" Baka chuckled as he glared at Reggie and Wendell. "I can assure you no one who has gone to this planet has ever returned."

"We can't wait." Wendell grimaced in anticipation. "And what about Sharkman?"

"I'm not quite finished with him. He and I have some important things to discuss before I'll have him join you."

As Baka reached out to cast his victims into a living hell, the captain's cabin was suddenly enveloped in ball of bright light.

"I can't see," Japapa yelled.

"Neither can I, you fool," Baka grumbled. "Grab Sharkman and the young men before they get away."

"Time to go," The Seer shouted to Sharkman and the youths. "I have momentarily blinded your tormenters, but it won't take them long to recover." After cutting the ropes that bound the trio, the voodoo priestess guided them into the black hole in the window of light. "Race toward the black void," the Seer urged.

Jumping up, Sharkman and the teens dove into the portal and ran as fast as they could. When Wendell looked behind him, Baka and Japapa had recovered their sight and were in swift pursuit. "Baka and Japapa are right behind us!" Wendell yelled as he fled toward the dark hole at the end of the tunnel of light.

"Good," The Seer chuckled. "That's just where I want them to be."

"But we'll never escape from dem." Reggie shouted when he looked back. "If dey follow us back ta our own time, we'll never be safe."

As they got closer to the black hole, the youths felt Baka and Japapa breathing down their necks and reaching out to grab them. It would only be a matter of seconds before the voodoo priest and Baka would have Sharkman and the boys within their grasp.

"Now!" The Seer shouted. "Jump into that black void. Fast!"

Fortune Island Reunion

As they leapt into the inky darkness, a brilliant flash of white light exploded behind them and Sharkman and the teens tumbled onto the beach of Fortune Island.

Shocked by the sudden appearance of their friends, Simone and Antonio stepped back in surprise. An elated Simone shouted, "Thank God you made it." When she recovered from the shock of their appearance, she raced toward her friends giving them each a huge hug as she began to cry with relief.

"Where's Antonio?" Sharkman asked after the joyful greetings were over.

"See for yourself," Simone smiled. "He's standing on the dune. I knew some Latin from my classes in school so I was able to communicate with him. I know he cares a great deal for you, Sharkman, and is probably very anxious to talk to you about this new world you have brought him to."

As Sharkman stepped over to be with Antonio, Wendell asked The Seer, "What happened to Baka and Japapa? I was certain they were going to catch up with us."

"That was never going to happen," The Seer chuckled. "I inserted them into a time bubble."

"What's dat?" Reggie asked and gave The Seer a puzzled look.

"It's a donut-shaped vacuum surrounded by a sphere of normal matter. Scientists call it a time machine. They will be trapped in this "time machine" and delivered to places far away from us."

"Is der any chance dey'll ever get out of dis time machine?"

"Yes," The Seer frowned, "but hopefully not for a very, very long time. If we're lucky they'll both be dumped back into that cauldron of fire you call Hell."

"Let's hope you're right about dat. Dos two keep showing up like de proverbial bad penny and we can't seem ta ever get rid of dem."

"Do you know if we've all been returned to Fortune Island about the same time Baka removed us from the island?" Simone asked.

Taking a moment to reflect upon Simone's question, The Seer said, "Not exactly, but you've been brought back close to the time that you were plucked from the cave. I should also tell you that for some of you your lives in this time line may have been altered somewhat, but I don't know by how much."

"Which means what?" Wendell asked.

"In all probability, your journeys into the past generated ripples in time which may have altered some of your previous lives. As a result, some things in this time line may not be exactly as they used to be."

"D-do you know what changes were generated?" Wendell stammered.

"Not all of them," The Seer responded, "but your journey through time has created a number of problems, which I'll try to correct as soon as possible. One of them involves Antonio, for example. Antonio and his family and coworkers were supposed to die when Vesuvius erupted, but when Sharkman rescued them and led them to safety in Capri, he caused a ripple in time which will change Sharkman's future. In order to avoid more changes, I'll need to return Antonio back to Capri as quickly as possible."

"How significant will those changes be?" Sharkman asked.

"I'm not sure. We will just have to wait and see."

"Will Sharkman's actions have any impact on de rest of us?" Reggie wanted to know.

"Only on yours, Reggie. In this time line, Japapa has never set up his drug-smuggling operation on Fortune Island and because he didn't, he would never have had any reason to kill your parents. So, it is distinctly possible that your parents might still be alive and they might still be planning to build their dream house on Fortune Island."

Staring at The Seer in a state of disbelief, Reggie tried to comprehend the fact that his parents might still be alive. It was too much for him to hope for.

"Right now, Mama Atabei and I have other things to attend to. However, before we do, I need to talk to Sharkman about preparing Antonio for his return to Capri. I know it will be difficult to convince the young man to return to his own time, but if Sharkman's life is ever going to return to what it was like before he left this island, the boy must be sent back to Capri. Even if I do this, Sharkman's life on this island may still have undergone considerable changes."

Sitting on the crest of a sand dune looking at the night sky, Sharkman explained to Antonio The Seer's plans to return him to Capri and gave the young man a friendly pat on the back and smiled. "This has been some journey for you and me. I imagine you missed your family while you've been gone?"

"I did," Antonio admitted. "It's also been hard for me to believe some of the things I've encountered. Do our Roman gods know about those monsters we'd met in the tropical forest and that gigantic ship we boarded with those terrible flying demons?"

"They probably do. Remember, The Seer said he was frequently in touch with your gods and told them all about the things he saw."

"Are our gods up there in the sky?" Antonio asked.

"Perhaps, but no one except The Seer and a few others have ever seen them. Some people believe that our gods live amongst that bright river of stars we see stretching across the night sky. We call that river of stars the Milky Way and it is filled with trillions of stars and planets."

"Has anyone from your time ever travelled to the Milky Way?" Looking at the seemingly endless stream of light, the young man smiled as he watched several meteorites streak across the heavens.

"No, but we have journeyed to the moon."

"Does anyone live there?" an astonished Antonio inquired.

"No, the people we sent there found no life on the moon. It was only a place full of rocks and dust, but enough questions for now. The Seer has just informed me that it's time for him to transport you back to your family in Capri." Standing up, Sharkman motioned for Antonio to follow him.

"Do I have to go?" Antonio asked.

"Yes. If my life is ever going to return to normal, you must leave. Even then, The Seer has told me that your departure may not account for all the changes he has seen in my future."

"Will you be coming back with me?" Antonio asked as he reluctantly followed Sharkman to the ocean's edge where The Seer was standing.

"Part way," he replied as the bright light from the portal embraced them.

The next thing Antonio knew, he was standing on the path that led to the village where his parents were staying. Turning around, he saw Sharkman and The Seer wave goodbye as the bright light of the portal faded away. Sharkman's departure would be one of the saddest moments in Antonio's life. However, he would never forget the old fisherman and the things he had learned from him. Looking up at the bright light of a full moon as it appeared from behind the clouds, he smiled and thought about what it must have been like for the first men that visited it.

Looking for the Treasure

"Everything is here and de engine seems ta be in good shape," Reggie shouted to Wendell and Simone who were watching him from the shore.

"You will find that most things have returned to the way they were before the hurricane transported all of you back in time," The Seer informed the youngsters. "However, in this time line, the people living on Crooked Island, including your families, never experienced the hurricane. For most of them, their lives continued on as if nothing has ever happened."

"You said most of the people's lives continued on as if nothing happened. What exactly does that mean?" Simone asked.

"You'll find the answer to that question yourselves in time. As I told you before, Mama Atabei and I must leave you at this point. There are more pressing things for us to do before we go our separate ways."

"What things?" Wendell asked. But before The Seer could respond, a bright light enveloped Mama Atabei and The Seer and they disappeared from view.

"I don't' like that The Seer and Mama Atabei took off so quickly. I would have liked to ask them more questions," Wendell said.

"Like what?" Simone asked.

"Like when Japapa will show up again."

"Why are you worried about that?" she asked. "The Seer already said he had taken care of them."

"I know, but I'm sure we haven't seen the end of those two."

"Have faith, I'm sure we won't have to worry about them," Simone replied as she bent over and kissed Wendell on the cheek and smiled. "I'm looking forward to our future."

When The Seer and Mama Atabei arrived in Haiti, The Seer turned to the priestess and said, "Sharkman has experienced a tragic life. He lost his family in a fire, spent a number of years in a Vietnamese prisoner of war camp, risked his life trying to save a sacred temple, and helped the teens escape from Japapa. Because of the things he's done to help other people and the tragic things that have happened in his life, I'm going to give him a special gift."

"I look forward to hearing what you have planned for him," Mama Atabei replied. "Now I must see what I can do for my homeland and its people."

"I should tell you before you leave," The Seer noted, "that the hurricane has never taken place in Haiti either. However, you will still have to deal with the impact of the earthquake on the island."

"I appreciate you telling me this. I would also like to thank you for the help you provided saving Sharkman and the youngsters."

"You're most welcome," The Seer responded as he waved goodbye and faded into the forest.

"Maybe we will meet again," were the last, faint words Mama Atabei heard from The Seer.

After Reggie finished checking his uncle's boat out, he scrambled over the side, waded to the beach, and returned to his companions.

"I was hoping ta find out more about my parents." Reggie sighed. "But now dat De Seer is gone I guess I will have ta discover de answers fer myself."

"What about the gold?" Wendell asked. "Do you think it's still here?"

"Gold?" Sharkman eyed the teens with suspicion.

"We weren't fishing fer lobsters wid your boat and my uncle's. We've been collecting gold, jewels and other precious objects from a sunken Spanish galleon off of Fortune Island before de hurricane struck," Reggie reluctantly admitted.

"And where is this treasure you've been accumulating?"

"Hopefully, in a cave nearby," Wendell said. "However, the treasure may no longer exist because of the ripples in time that we've generated. I think we should check the cave out to see if our treasure is still there."

"Do you mind if I tag along?" Sharkman asked.

"Of course not," Simone said, "especially since we intended to give you a portion of the fortune we've uncovered."

Upon reaching the cave entrance, Simone planted herself on a rock and said, "Go ahead, I'll wait for you here. I hope the treasure we collected is still there."

Giving her a curious look, Sharkman asked, "What's the matter? Why aren't you coming?"

"She's afraid of de bats and de roaches living inside de cave," Reggie laughed.

Glaring at Reggie, Simone folded her hands across her chest and snapped, "And I suppose nothing frightens you, like Baka's idea of tossing you overboard to become shark meat?"

"That's enough bickering," Sharkman said. "If she doesn't want to go inside, let her be. Let's go in and check out the place where you hid the treasure."

"We stored it on a ledge behind some rocks a short distance from the entrance so no one could find it," Wendell told Sharkman.

Racing ahead, Reggie clamored up to the rocky ledge in the cave, and shouted to his friends, "It's all here. As far as I can tell, nothing is missing."

When Sharkman climbed up the ledge and entered the cave where the treasure had been stored, he was shocked by the huge quantity of gold and jewels the youngsters had collected and whistled in amazement. "This is incredible. My guess is that you've retrieved millions of dollars in gold and jewels, maybe even more. Of course, you will have to give at least a portion of what you found to the Bahamian government."

"I wasn't planning on giving dem anything," Reggie grumbled. "Dey haven't done anything ta deserve part of dis treasure. One thing's fer sure; you certainly know how ta dampen a person's enthusiasm."

"I understand, but that's the law and there's nothing any of us can do to change it. I'll tell you what; I'll talk to some lawyers I know in Nassau and see what kind of settlement they can reach with the government. Even if you get half of what's here, you'll all become millionaires. My guess is that you'll get several million each. You have to admit that's an awful lot of money, certainly enough for you to fulfill any dreams you ever had. In the meantime, I suggest moving this treasure to a safer place until all the legal transactions regarding who gets what are completed."

"All right," Reggie grumbled. "But I'll need some time ta figure out a safer place ta move it ta."

"That's fine," Sharkman acknowledged. "Now let's head back to the beach. I'd like to get to my fishing camp. I'm also sure Reggie would like to learn what changes have taken place in his life."

"I agree," Wendell said with an enthusiastic nod.

When they reached the beach, Reggie swam out to the boat, started up the engine and motioned to Simone, Wendell and Sharkman to wade out and climb on board.

"Thanks for the offer of a ride," the old fisherman said. "It'll save me a long walk home."

After clamoring aboard the boat, Sharkman perched himself on the bow and smiled. His journey back in time was over and Baka and Japapa were no longer a threat. Soon, he would be enjoying a peaceful night's sleep in his hut and tomorrow he would look for his boat and enjoy a full day of fishing on the reef.

As Reggie's uncle's boat skimmed across the clear, blue-green water, everyone took some time to relax. Basking in the cool breeze and salt spray generated by the boat as it raced across the tranquil waters, they watched a cluster of puffy clouds begin to merge and form a late afternoon thunderstorm over Fortune Island. It had been a terrifying and stressful adventure for the youngsters and they couldn't wait to return to their families and find out what had happened while they were away.

As Simone sat next to Wendell, she looked at her friend with concern. "Do you think our efforts to collect the treasure from the Spanish galleon were worth the terrible experiences we've been through and the ordeal Sharkman was subjected to?"

"I don't know. What are you thinking?" Wendell asked.

"I've thought a lot about it and only hope some good comes from it all."

"Like what?"

"Like Reggie being able to build his house on Fortune Island, Sharkman saving the temple in Vietnam, and my father being able to use the money to help people in Haiti."

"We'll just have to make sure our treasures are used wisely," Wendell responded.

"I'm glad you feel that way. I'm counting on you to help make it happen," Simone said as she took hold of Wendell's hand and smiled.

Capri—Antonio and His Dad

"I'm glad we escaped to Capri," Antonio said as he took the helm from his father and guided their fishing boat back to port.

"I am too," his father replied as he scanned the moonlit water trying to make sure his son didn't encounter any hidden structures below the surface. "I'm curious. Did you ever find out where the old fisherman ran off to?" his father asked. "I often wonder if he escaped from the people that were after him and has found a place where they can't find him."

"I'm certain that he did." Antonio smiled. "When I finally caught up with him on the trail leading out of town, he assured me he had discovered a place where the people who were after him would never find where he was hiding out.

"That's good. It means a lot to me to know he's safe. He did a lot for us. If it wasn't for him, none of us would be alive today."

"I know." Antonio sighed. The young man looked back at the large haul of fish on the deck and grinned. "If we keep making hauls of fish like this, we'll soon become wealthy enough to build a home for ourselves on the hillside."

Giving his son's shoulder a squeeze, Julius smiled. "I agree. With the amount of fish we're catching it won't take long."

After they pulled alongside their dock and tied the boat up, Antonio looked up into the sky and smiled. "Sometime in the distant future, I believe people from this planet will visit the moon."

"I doubt it," Julius laughed. "Only our gods have the power to do something like that."

"Don't be so sure." Antonio replied. "I'm certain someday people like us will walk on its surface."

Giving his son an odd look, Julius began shoveling their catch into some wooden containers on the dock. Since his son had returned from his last encounter with Sharkman, he had begun telling him strange stories about giant reptiles, flying demons and time travel. He didn't know what had induced this kind of thinking in the boy, but he was hoping it was just a passing phase he was going through. Julius was worried about the boy and thought: *If he continues to tell stories like the ones he is telling us and his friends, people will soon begin to think he's crazy.*

Antonio just laughed because he was sure he knew differently.

Surprises

"Is that your house?" Wendell asked as their boat approached the place where Sharkman's hut was supposed to be located.

Looking at the elegant home situated near the beach, Sharkman laughed and said, "I doubt it. I couldn't afford a palace like that. I'm sure my meager living quarters are a little further down the beach."

"Well, either some high class neighbors have moved next door ta you or one of dos ripples in time has enhanced your living quarters," Reggie chuckled.

"I don't see how that's possible," a perplexed Sharkman replied. "The Seer said he'd returned us to Fortune Island at approximately the same time we left."

"Yeah," Reggie laughed. "He also told us dat because of de ripples in time Antonio created, we might find some things have changed, like de fact dat my parents are now alive."

"Well, it looks like someone has taken possession of the place where you used to live," Simone said. "Look. They even built a fancy dock extending into the lagoon. Why don't we tie up and see who your new neighbors are."

When the boat was secured to the dock, a strange woman waved and walked toward their boat.

"Does anyone know who she is?" Simone asked.

"Not de slightest," Reggie said as Sharkman and Wendell nodded their heads in agreement.

After the group climbed onto the dock, a slender woman with beautiful, flowing black hair and blue eyes approached Sharkman and gave him a big hug and kiss. "Welcome back," the woman said with a worried look. "You've been gone so long I had begun to get concerned about you."

More than a little confused, the teens stared at Sharkman and the woman in shock. Ultimately, it was Simone who decided how to find out who the woman was without asking her directly. "I hope we didn't keep Sharkman away too long," she said with a look of regret.

"Oh no, Simone. My father loves going out fishing with you. It's just that this trip seemed to take much longer than usual. My only regret is that his grandson, Antonio, couldn't go with you. Would you like to come up to the house for some refreshments before you head back to Landrail? I've got some fine lemonade I prepared earlier, and it would give you a chance to tell Antonio all about your fishing trip."

"Sure," Reggie replied, still trying to get a handle on the whole situation. *Maybe we could get more information about this family while we sit around a table chatting and drinking lemonade*, he thought to himself as they walked toward the house.

As they approached the marble structure, Sharkman and the teens stared at the exquisite entrance with their mouths agape. The walkway lead up to two ornately carved wooden doors that were surrounded by a beautiful landscaped garden filled with numerous species of colorful wildflowers, and on each side of the path there were two tall, water fountains. Following the woman through the entry doors, they entered a dome-shaped hallway whose walls and ceiling were painted with tropical Bahamian scenes that surrounded an atrium filled with colorful finches.

"Mom always loved finches," Sharkman's daughter laughed. "And when you offered to build mom a home in the Bahamas where you lived, you told her you would create one of the most beautiful atriums she had ever seen."

Sharkman said, "I'm glad I was able to please her."

"Mom said that when you visited Capri after the war and she saw you for the first time, it was love at first sight. You told her you had visited the island once before and fell in love with it. You said you wanted to return and see what changes had taken place. Not wanting you to get away, she invited you to her family's house on the hill for dinner. After that, your romance moved along quite quickly, and you were married a year later. Almost everyone on the island came to the wedding and mom's father paid for this house in the Bahamas as a wedding gift. Please head into the kitchen," she said, pointing down the hallway. "Antonio is having his dinner there and most certainly will be happy to see all of you, especially since he didn't get a chance to go out fishing with you."

Heading down the hallway, Sharkman surveyed his surroundings and thought how much the house reminded him of a Roman palace. He really must have made an impression on his father-in-law for him to pay the cost of building a home of this quality for his family. Interested in finding out if his wife was still living he asked his daughter, "Is your mother home?"

"Heavens no. Valaria has gone to the airport and taken the Wednesday flight to Nassau. She's purchasing some supplies we needed, but she's promised to be back by Friday."

"I'm glad to see she will be back soon. I'm always anxious when she's away. I'll certainly be glad to see her."

As the group stepped into the kitchen, Antonio turned around and smiled at the old man.

"Grandpa," the boy shouted as he pushed back his chair and raced to greet Sharkman.

This can't be true, Sharkman thought to himself as the boy wrapped his arms around him. *My grandson looks exactly like the boy Antonio I just sent back to Capri.*

Simone, Reggie and Wendell couldn't believe what they were seeing either. After taking a seat at the table, they continued to stare at one another in amazement.

"Mom has made some lemonade," Antonio said. "Would you like some?"

After nodding their heads, Antonio hurried to the refrigerator and brought back a full pitcher.

"Does your mother frequently fly to Nassau?" Wendell asked as he poured himself a glass of the refreshing liquid.

Valaria flies there about every two weeks," Juliana responded. "She uses Bahamas Air to travel back and forth."

"Juliana, I'm a bit curious why you and your husband named your son Antonio?" Simone asked.

"Funny you should ask. Dad insisted that we name our first child after a good friend he once knew. Ironically, it's also a name that frequently appears in our family history that goes back to Roman times. So when Sharkman heard that my husband and I were going to call our first son Antonio, he was elated."

"I'm sorry to interrupt this conversation, but I think we should get going and let Sharkman get some dinner," Wendell said.

Simone added, "We're also anxious to get back to Landrail; we don't want Reggie's uncle and our parents worrying about us. As you said, we've been gone a long time."

"I understand," Juliana replied as she retrieved their empty glasses and placed them in the dish washer. Walking the teens to the door, she waved goodbye as they hastily retreated down the wooden dock.

When the trio got to the boat, Simone shook her head and said, "I think we all have a lot of catching up to do, especially Sharkman. I can't wait to hear the stories he'll have to tell us the next time we see him."

"Neither can we," Reggie and Wendell agreed.

"Now, let's find out what's waiting fer de rest of us when we get ta Landrail," Reggie said with anticipation. Starting up the motor, he pointed the boat toward the Crooked Island mainland and smiled.

As Reggie pulled the boat up to his uncle's dock in Landrail, he was greeted by one of his longtime friends, Paul, who had just come back from a lobster fishing trip. "Hi, Reggie," he said with a smile. "Looks like you got back just in time for de party."

"What party?" Reggie asked.

"De one your folks are hosting at Gibson's ta celebrate de loan dey got ta build a new home on Fortune Island. Everyone's der including Wendell's folks, his grandfather, and Simone's parents and brother.

The news was almost too much for Reggie to imagine. The Seer had said something like this might happen but it was hard for him to believe. The fact that his folks were still alive when he returned home was difficult for him to comprehend. That wrinkle in time that Antonio had created had certainly had a wonderful impact on his and Sharkman's lives.

"Let's head up and join the party," Simone said. "I'm eager to see everyone." Taking hold of Reggie's and Wendell's hands, they raced to the restaurant to see what changes had taken place among their families and friends. "After seeing what has happened to Sharkman, the story your folks will have to tell us should really be a whopper," Simone chuckled.

When Reggie stepped into the restaurant, he stared at his parents. The fact that they were alive remained hard for him to accept.

"Reggie!" his mother shouted and waved as he walked up to the table. "Your father and I were worried dat you wouldn't make it ta de celebration in time. Take a seat and have your friends sit down and join us. I assume you heard our good news. We received de loan ta build our home on Fortune Island and if all goes well, we hope ta begin construction in about a month."

"Dat's great," Reggie responded. "I can't wait fer you ta get started."

"Neither can we," Reggie's father said. "And just think, Sharkman and his family are going ta be our neighbors."

"We couldn't believe it when de bank called us yesterday and told us dat our application fer de loan had gone through," Reggie's mother said excitedly. "And you know what de most fantastic thing was?"

"What's dat?" Reggie asked.

"De bank manager dat pushed our loan through told us de most fascinating story. He said his whole family was brought ta de Bahamas as slaves. He said his great, great, great grandfather was sold ta a mine owner from Bonaire and was about ta be shipped ta de island when a young man named Reggie freed him. When we told him our son's name was Reggie, it sealed de deal. He said he couldn't deny a loan ta anyone whose son was named after de man dat rescued his grandfather. Can you imagine dat!"

Speechless, Reggie turned and looked at Simone and Wendell who were both staring at him with their mouths agape.

Future Decisions

Sharkman was slowly getting accustomed to his new lifestyle when his wife Valaria entered from the kitchen and informed him that there was a handsome man standing on the dock who wanted to see him.

"Did he tell you his name?"

"Yes. He said his name is Robert Sims. He told me his father was the former captain aboard an aircraft carrier that you once visited."

Smiling, Sharkman stood up and said, "Well, let's not make him wait. Invite him in."

"Then you know him?"

"No. But I had a brief encounter with his father during the war. I suspected that one day someone in the Sims family might try to get in contact with me."

"Are you concerned?"

"No, his father was just a brief acquaintance and the young man probably has a lot of questions he wants to ask me."

As Robert entered the living room, Sharkman had to agree with his wife. The young man was quite good looking. The man's six-foot, muscular frame, salt and pepper hair and rugged facial features reminded him of his father. Reaching out, Sharkman shook the man's hand and invited him to sit down in one of the wicker rocking chairs in their living room. "I've found these seats quite comfortable, especially as I get older," Sharkman said.

"It's nice to meet you, Robert," Valaria said. "You'll have to excuse me but I need to finish cleaning up in the kitchen."

After relaxing in the chair, Robert smiled and said, "You don't look a day older than the picture my father took of you when the two of you met on his aircraft carrier. Your house is beautiful. Someday, I hope to live on an island like this. You seem to have done quite well for yourself after living through your ordeals in the prison camp."

"Yes. I have. But I'll have to admit I can't take any credit for this wealth I've acquired. Valaria's father built this house for us as a wedding gift. And your father? How has life treated him?" Sharkman inquired.

"He passed away several years ago. Thanks for asking though," Robert said. "He retired as a four-star admiral and I'm happy to say lived a comfortable life until he passed.

But the one thing he couldn't let go of when you and the others disappeared was whether or not time travel was really possible."

"And now you know the answer," Sharkman smiled.

"I do. And if you don't mind telling me, where are the others you were travelling with?"

"Antonio has returned to Capri to be with his family and The Seer and Mama Atabei are in Haiti."

"And the friends you were anxious to save? Were you successful?"

"Yes. In fact I just went fishing with them the other day. There is one thing I would like to ask you: what happened to the sacred temple my men and I discovered in the jungle?" Sharkman asked. "When I was discharged from the military, I could never find any information about it in books or in the declassified reports that my friends passed along to me."

"I suspected you might want to know about the temple." Robert sat back in the rocking chair and smiled. "The government has managed to keep its location a secret just as you requested and the priests still visit it once a year. Over the last few years, they have begun warning us about the terrible things that are about to take place on our planet because of global warming."

"I would take their warnings seriously," Sharkman said with a look of concern.

"We do. And that's the primary reason I stopped by to visit you today. The government needs your help and the help of your friends. If we don't stop accelerated global warming soon, billions of people will die and the world's economy will be in shambles. Because of the interest my father generated in me about time travel, I've spent the last twenty years or so of my life creating a time machine that will enable us to travel into both the past and the future. I know most scientists tell us that time travel is impossible, but, of course, we both know differently. In order to stop this threat from global warming, the government has developed a device that will eliminate the impact of accelerated global warming, but we'll need your help to activate it.

"Using my time machine, I helped the government transport the device into the future. Since you and your friends are the only people I know who have ever experienced time travel, and your group are the only ones that understand the problems people can generate when undertaking such a trip, we felt you would be the most qualified individuals to take on this task for us. Consequently, we want you and your friends to go into the future and use a tracking device we've developed to locate the government's equipment, make some minor repairs to it, and trigger the operating switches."

Sharkman sat back in his chair for several minutes and thought about the young man's proposal. "I've always thought that when I got old, retired life would allow me to enjoy the fruits of my labor. If I hear you correctly, and my friends and I don't help you with this task, and we don't activate this device, our families and many others will be threatened with extinction?"

"Yes. I'm afraid so. Please take some time to think about my request. Talk about it amongst your friends, but under no circumstances should you or your friends tell anyone else about what we discussed here."

"Of course," Sharkman said thinking over the implications of what the young man had told him. "However, there are many components of your request you seem reluctant to reveal."

"At this point, I can't say anything else," Robert said and stood up. "I'll be heading back this way in about a week to hear what you're decision is. I'm really hoping you will agree to help us."

Standing up, Robert Sims shook Sharkman's hand and stepped into the kitchen to say goodbye to Valaria.

"Your friend seems worried about something," Valaria observed as she watched Robert leave.

"He is," Sharkman nodded. "And he has left me with a very tough decision to make."

"I'm sick of travelling through parallel universes in this time machine," Japapa grouched.

"I don't like it any more than you do," Baka retorted, "especially when I have to spend it with an incompetent fool like you. By the way do you still have that locket I gave you?"

"Yes, why do you want to know?"

"It may provide us with a way to escape the predicament we're in."

Once we escape this time chamber and return to Hell, I can assure you I'll make certain that I dump you back into that boiling pit of tar for the rest of eternity and find a way to get my revenge on The Seer and his friends. I can also assure you, that this time they will suffer in more ways than you can imagine."

"I've heard you spout those promises before," Japapa laughed, "and I'm beginning to think that you're no more capable of carrying out your threats against them or on some of the other scoundrels you've encountered."

"We'll see," Baka snarled. "Now would you please return the locket and stop wasting my time."

"Certainly," Japapa smiled. "I don't want to waste your time trying to get us out of this predicament. Perhaps after I give the locket to you, you'll reconsider tossing me back into a cauldron of boiling tar."

"Perhaps. I have to admit you have been of some use to me."

"Thanks," Japapa grinned.

"By the way, what are your plans for the temple Sharkman discovered?"

"The temple is the least of my problems after we get out of here," Baka grumbled. "The device the U.S. government has created to eliminate accelerated global warming worries me even more at the moment."